Murder on the Italian Tour

Death has been Added to the Itinerary

John V. Noonan

Published by:
John V. Noonan
1005 Aurora Way
Wheaton, Illinois

ISBN   978-0-9996482-1-6

October 2021

For Grant, Evan, Alex, Sadie, and Hudson

PART ONE

Chapter 1

Chicago

Wednesday, May 15, 2019

Becca

Lufthansa Flight 567 to Frankfurt sat on the O'Hare runway for about 25 minutes before taking off. The 5:30 Flight was behind schedule and would probably be late to Frankfurt. Chicago was having a normal summer thunderstorm, and the plane was waiting for the weather to clear enough for a takeoff. Becca Park looked out from her window seat, hoping for a sudden switchover to blue sky. But it didn't come. Instead, the jet took off and climbed through the clouds. Minor turbulence shook the plane as it banked to the northeast, causing Becca to grip her armrests. Her husband, David, sat in the aisle of the 2-4-2 configuration. He put his hand on Becca's and said, "Relax, will you? You took your pill, didn't you?"

The pill was her dose of Clonazepam. Becca used it to reduce her anxiety when flying. She had always been a hesitant flyer, but, lately, her fears had gotten worse. Clonazepam seemed to work, and it had become a standard component of her travel plans. She and David had taken several trips within the past few years: London, Hawaii, and Amsterdam. Now they were on their way to Rome, with a first leg stopover in Frankfurt, Germany. They would spend several days

1

in Rome and then go down to Sorrento, about an hour south of Naples. Sorrento was their target destination. From there they would pick up their 10-day Kastner Tour of Italy.

The plane bounced again, and Becca clutched tighter. She blinked her eyes and looked sideways at David. "I did, but it mustn't have kicked in yet."

David gave a perfunctory, "OK", and turned back to his in-seat video screen.

Becca thought about the pills in her purse. The prescription was for five pills, the same as for her other long flights. One to get there, one to get back, and several extra ones in case of flight delays or missed connections.

All five were still in her purse.

Now she would have to really suppress her fears. She had to act like she had taken the pill, at least enough to convince David. It was 90 minutes since she was supposed to have taken the pill, and, if David had been paying any attention, he would have noticed the extended time. Clonazepam normally was taken when the flight was called at the gate. Then, it would kick in by the time they were settled for take-off. Still, she wasn't surprised that David hadn't noticed. She felt like it was fitting the pattern of his lack of attention to anything having to do with her.

The view out her window suddenly cleared, and she again became hopeful that the bouncing would stop. She glanced upward and saw another layer of thick, gray clouds. In very short time, the plane would shake its way through another tough patch of nasty clouds. She let out a slow breath, and decided to try the breathing techniques she used before the Clonazepam.

She looked out at the tip of the wing to establish a focal point. Then she counted backwards from a hundred, with a slow exhale at each number, trying to will herself, or convince herself, that she was twice as relaxed as for the previous number. With each decrement, she consciously tried to relax her muscles. As the window went dark again, she was at 93. It wasn't working. She felt a prolonged vibration and decided to start over again. She was a wreck.

But she told herself she wasn't going to use her Clonazepam. She was saving them for a better purpose. She would just have to endure the flight.

When they finally broke through the upper clouds, the sun was setting behind her, and she had a clear view of the clouds below. Her view across the clouds was unlimited. That would help. The ride began to smooth, and the plane started a slow ascent. The captain came over the speakers and welcomed everyone to the flight. He apologized for the bumpy climb through the clouds and announced their flight time to Frankfurt. Their cruising altitude would be 39,000 feet. They would probably be just a little late but would try to make up for the delay. Becca knew from her previous flights that she could expect a relatively smooth flight. They shouldn't hit any weather issues until at least they hit England or continental Europe. At 40,000 feet and an outside temperature of 50 below, there wasn't enough variation in the air to cause any air turbulence.

She glanced back at the sunset. Now she would only have to deal with the darkness. And the fact they would be in the darkness over water – the icy Atlantic. She closed her eyes and dropped her chin to her chest.

Then she began to count backwards again.

When the sunlight was completely gone, she lost sight of the clouds and the distance. The moon was absent. She could make out the blinking red light on the tip of the wing, but, beyond its flashing, she saw only total blackness and obscurity. The red light became her new focal point. She imagined that it was a light on the ground and that she was really only just off the ground. But her thoughts then turned to the realization that she was eight miles above the frozen tundra of Canada. Or was it now the blackened abyss of the North Atlantic? And she was hurtling through space at 500 miles per hour. She imagined what would happen if they crashed into the tundra. She figured that they would all die on impact. Or, if they went into the ocean? Then, she reasoned, they would all either freeze in the water or drown in a sunken plane. She figured that the first sign of trouble would be some kind of sudden movement or shaking of the plane. So, she sat there in anticipation, and dread, of the slightest sign of turbulence. She looked over at David. His movie was still playing, but he was sound asleep. She wanted to slam his head into the screen.

There was nothing she could do but sit in excruciating panic for the next several hours. So that is what she did. She told herself, over and over again, that it would all be worth it.

And she envisioned her return flight back to Chicago, loaded up on Clonazepam, with her husband David safely secured in a casket in the cargo hold.

Chapter 2

Zurich

Thursday, May 16, 2019

Mellow

Melody O'Neal was certain that her boss was going to fire her. She had thought it through and, given her own experience as a Human Resources Manager, it all made sense. He called the meeting for a Thursday, not Friday. You never fire anyone on a Friday. It was set for 8:00 AM. You never fire anyone at the end of the day; you do it early in the morning to get it over with. It is too awkward to have the person around all day when you, as the manager, know you are going to let them go. And she had created enough drama on the recent Rhine River Cruise to set everyone on edge. Her boss had already coached her multiple times about trying to get along better with her coworkers, but she couldn't hold her tongue on the last cruise. She had argued again with her coworkers, the chef, and the captain. Yep, today would be the day she would be fired.

She stopped just before stepping onto the Munsterbrucke Bridge. The double towers of the Grossmunster Church, Zurich's most famous landmark, stood just across the river. She eyed it briefly, but her gaze quickly shifted to the small white office building just across the street from the church. Her destination was the third floor, where Kastner Tours had their Zurich office. She was a bit early, but she began her trudge across the bridge. Since she was going to get fired, she might as well get it over with.

She paused halfway across the bridge and looked up again at the Grossmunster. She thought that, once she was fired, maybe she'd finally take the time to climb the steps. What else would she have to do today? The Church has been there for 800 years and it is not going anywhere. But she has lived here in Zurich for three years and never taken the time to climb the 200 steps to the top. She decided: that's what she'd do later this morning.

And, while she was looking for a new job, she would have time to do more digging into who her father really was. That issue came up at his funeral back in February. Her efforts so far had been fruitless.

Her meeting started early. By 7:45 she found herself sitting across from her boss, Luca Keller. He offered coffee. She declined. He tried to engage in some pleasantries, but she saw an unhappy smile on his face. She folded her arms across her chest, sat back and said, "OK, I'm here. What do you want to talk about?"

Luca took a slow sip of his coffee. "Mellow, we need to discuss last week's river cruise."

She was surprised he used her nickname, but she waited for him to go on.

"I've gotten some telephone calls and some emails. I understand that you had some … disagreements … first with the chef and then the captain himself. And then the other Tour Directors on the riverboat." He paused. "We have talked about this. You are one of my best Tour Directors. The guests always love you, but you can't seem to get along with anyone else who works here at Kastner Tours."

"Well, if people would just do their jobs, we would all get along OK. What did the chef complain about?"

"He said that you were telling him how to cook the breakfasts."

Mellow leaned forward. "He was using *pooled* eggs!"

"He told me that's what you argued about. He assured me that they are legal and safe."

"Do you even know what pooled eggs are?"

"Yes, but I don't think you will be happy until you explain it, so go ahead."

"It's when you crack a dozen or so eggs and mix them together for omelets, or scrambled eggs, or even French toast. The problem is that if even one egg is bad, then the whole batch gets infected. If even one of the eggs is bad, it is a sure-fire way to spread salmonella to dozens of people."

"He told me that it is legal and safe. And that most restaurants and ships do it."

"Did he tell you about the recalls in Germany and Italy?" Mellow could tell from the reaction on his face that the chef had not shared the recall information.

"What recalls?"

"They were on *organic* eggs in Germany and Italy. They were positive for salmonella. It happened last month. Do you remember the 2016 breakout of salmonella? In the Netherlands and Belgium? And Luxembourg? You would think that a chef, of all people, would be taking special precautions."

"So, you went into the kitchen and complained to him about it?"

"I went to talk with him about it, and I told him it wasn't safe. That he was putting the health of our guests at risk."

"What did he say?"

"He didn't take too kindly to it. And he told me, quote, to get the hell out of my kitchen."

Luca pursed his lips. "What happened with Captain Baxter? He said that in Cologne you were out with guests and came back over an hour late. And it wasn't even an official excursion. He said that because of your tardiness, the boat left the dock late and was then late to the next port. Because you weren't back in time."

"I can explain that."

"Please do."

Mellow took a measured breath. "I took a group to the NS Documentation Center."

"You couldn't go to the Botanical Gardens?" He shook his head. "Or the Chocolate Museum? You took them to a Nazi prison?"

"We had a morning walking tour that ended around noon. Then the guests had free time until our 4:00 departure. One of them asked about the Center."

"So, you took it upon yourself to take him?"

"Well, there were eight in all. Mr. Cooperman, his wife, and three other couples. He wanted to go because his uncle was killed there. And his father was tortured there. He didn't find out until last year, when his father finally told him about the War. Then his father died a few months later. He felt a need to go there. Have you ever been there?"

"No, I haven't."

"It's a very … moving experience. I went with them because there were eight of them and I thought my German would come in handy. It did. I have been there many times, and I was able to supplement the audio guide."

"So why were you late to the boat?"

"It takes several hours to go through it properly. I tried to move them along, but it was a tough experience for him. He was overcome and needed time. I called Frederick to tell him we might be late. And it just took a while to get back. I kept Frederick informed of our situation." Mellow thought that using the Lead Tour Director's name would help her situation.

"And you had words with Captain Baxter?"

"He was waiting for us when we returned, and he took me aside. I told him what happened. I guess you could say we *had words*. It got a little heated."

"The boats have to be on time. He was not happy at all."

"I get that. But the reality is that if I had not gone with them, they would have been even later."

Luca stood up and walked over to his window. Mellow could see that Luca knew she was right about an unaccompanied group being even later. She thought it best to suppress her urge to keep talking. It was hard, but she figured it was Luca's move now. There were several moments of silence as Luca's eyes stayed focused on something beyond the window.

Finally, he turned back to Mellow. "Well, here's where I am at. I have a very hard time assigning you to tours because there is always some incident or drama with our other staff. The guests love you. I know that. But you never seem to let others do their job."

Mellow launched, "Well, if they …" Then she stopped. "Sorry."

"We have a situation in Italy. You may have heard about Melanie."

Melanie was a fellow Tour Director who was expecting her first child in July. "No, I haven't. Is she OK?"

"Nothing has really happened, but her doctor has put her on bed rest until she delivers. Just a precaution, but something she has to do. It complicates our scheduling."

"I've done Italy a dozen times. I know it well."

"I can give you this final chance. I need you to fill in for her. But nothing, and I mean *nothing* can go wrong. The driver, the local guides, the hotels, restaurants, or anything. You need to start trusting your co-workers. When you trust people, they will often surprise you. When people know they are not trusted, they tune you out."

Mellow saw reluctance in Luca's expression and tone of voice. She sensed that he did not expect her to be able to do it. To run a tour without some kind of drama that would escalate to his office. And Mellow realized that, were it not for Melanie's situation, she likely would have been fired today. The corollary was that this Italy tour could easily be her last assignment with Kastner Tours.

"I can assure you that nothing will go wrong. I will get along with everyone. Which tour is it? When does it start?"

"It's the *Best of* tour. Northbound. It starts on Sunday night."

"Sunday night! Luca, that's three days away. I have to be in Sorrento on Sunday?"

He tilted his head slightly and gave a half-smile. "If I were you, I would leave for Sorrento today. I will have Sheila send you the details and logistics. Check your email."

It was clear in his tone that the meeting was over. It had to be the quickest meeting she had ever had with Luca. He was known for, first, being late all of the time, and second, for droning on and running over. Often unmercifully. She took his shortness as a bad sign.

She stood to leave. Luca stopped her with, "One more thing."

"What's that?"

"How in the world did your ever get the nickname *Mellow*? Because you certainly *are not*."

Chapter 3

Sorrento

Saturday, May 18, 2019

Mellow

Mellow got to The Olivian hotel late in the afternoon. She pulled her spinner into the room and surveyed her surroundings. The bellman should arrive soon with her other luggage. It wasn't a premium room; those were reserved for the tour guests. But it was functional; a queen bed, a television, a modest sitting area, and a private bath. Per her normal routine she checked the bathroom.

It looked bright and clean. She looked behind the door and flinched. Along the wall behind the door, she saw several strands of black hair and a couple of dust-bunnies. She bent over for a closer inspection. She grabbed a tissue, walked directly to the telephone, and, with her fingers safely protected, dialed the front desk. It rang once.

"*Buongiorno, Signorina* O'Neal."

"*Buongiorno.* English please?"

"Yes, of course. How many I help you?

"I have just checked in and this room will not do. It is not very clean. The bathroom floor needs attention."

"I am very sorry about that. I can send the Housekeeping staff right away."

"No, I'm sorry. That won't do. Is Mr. Garzanelli available?"

There was a pause. Giovanni Garzanelli was the Hotel Manager.

"Yes, of course. I will ring him. Do you want to hold or should I have him call you back?"

"I will hold. *Grazie.*"

"*Prego.*"

She only had to wait a couple of minutes.

"Good afternoon, Ms. O'Neal. I understand that your room is less than satisfactory. We can move you to another room, if you like."

"Thank you, Giovanni." She used his first name to personalize the interaction. They had known each other for many years. The Olivian was the first choice of Kastner Tours for any business or events in Sorrento, and Mellow has stayed there at least 20 times. Whenever they hosted a Kastner group, Giovanni always sought her out to personally greet her. And, at the end, he always checked with her for feedback on the hotel's performance.

"Please give me a couple of minutes. I will personally inspect the room before we move you."

"That will be great. I will come down to the lobby. Can you make sure the other rooms are clean? I don't want any of my tour guests to experience the same thing."

"But of course. I will have the Housekeeping Manager personally check each room. I did not realize that you were arriving. I thought Miss Melanie was conducting the tour."

She thought about explaining that Melanie was on bed rest, but decided that it was Melanie's news, not hers. "No, you have me this tour."

"Well, if I had known you were coming, I would have checked the room myself ahead of time. None of the other Tour Directors are as …", he let out a soft chuckle, "… thorough … as you are."

"Thorough." Mellow laughed aloud. "That's a nice way of putting it, Giovanni. I will have to remember that word. Oh, and can you also check to make sure that each of the guestrooms has washcloths? They are Americans, you know."

"Certainly."

Within the hour, Mellow was settled in her room. It had been cleaned well.

Giovanni had sent an apologetic bottle of Brunello to her room, and she carried it with her on her way to the rooftop restaurant, Olivia's View.

Entering the restaurant, she walked past two rows of potted lemon trees and found her way to the open-air dining area. She had been to Olivia's View many times, but each time she emerged to see the view from the rooftop, she shook her head at the sight. Directly ahead she looked across the crystal blue Bay of Naples. She saw dramatic splotches of various shades of turquoise. There were no obstructions and she felt like she was right on top of the water. To her right she saw the imposing Mt. Vesuvius, pushing up as a solitary sentinel for the Bay. Light, passing clouds cast moving shadows across Vesuvius. She felt a slight, salty breeze on her face. Her eye caught several seagulls in formation over the bay. A pelican dove for his meal. She saw the muted splash and swore she could hear the water splatter. In an instant it was all gone and she couldn't tell where the pelican entered the water.

It was captivating, and Mellow easily understood why The Olivian charged top euro for the restaurant. And why everyone paid it.

She allowed herself a few minutes of gawking. Then she sat at a table, near the old stone railing, and began to get to work. A server arrived and opened her wine.

She spread out her materials. This would be her final run-through for the tour. She began with the itinerary. Tonight, reception at Olivia's View. That will be a spectacular beginning.

Tomorrow, Monday, a drive and tour of the Amalfi Coast.

Tuesday would be Pompeii, lunch in Naples, and then on to Rome. Wednesday and Thursday would be Rome. Assisi on Friday. Florence on Saturday and Sunday. And, finally, Monday and Tuesday in Venice.

When she left the Kastner offices in Zurich on Thursday, her intention was to go directly to Sorrento on Friday. But she re-thought her plans. She figured it would be better to stay in Zurich on Friday to make all of her phone calls to confirm the plans for the tour. Better to do that on Friday so that any issues she identified could be addressed before the Sunday start of the tour. She had to make sure that nothing went wrong on the tour. Everything had to be buttoned up. Then, on Saturday, she flew to Naples and took a car service to The Olivian.

She had called to finalize plans with The Olivian, the local guides for each of their stops, the restaurants for lunches and dinners, and the featured speakers in Florence and Venice. She saw that several of the local guides were unfamiliar names. She tried to call the driver of the coach, but ended up leaving a voice message. She chuckled at his name – Angelo Michaels. She knew of him but had not been with him on a tour. She figured his name would be a running joke during the tour; and she tried to think of some clever way to use his name to break the ice with him and start to have some kind of friendly dialogue. Maybe she could call him Michelangelo during the tour, and the guests would go back home and be able to say, "Yes, Michelangelo drove us through Italy for ten days." She had scanned the guest list to see if any were marked as vegan or vegetarian. Happily, there were none. That made the tour easier for her, with much less likelihood that a complaint would escalate to Luca's desk,

She took a small sip of her Brunello. It was terrific; dry, full-bodied, a base of blackberry, and the right amount of earthy expresso. She pulled out her notes and quickly ensured that they were all in her folder: Lemons in Sorrento and Amalfi, Salerno landing in World War II, Pompeii, Michelangelo, DaVinci, Roman emperors, Colosseum, The Vatican, St. Francis of Assisi, Vineyards in Tuscany, Florence, Ponte Vecchio Bridge, the Medici, Bonfire of the Vanities, Uffizi, Venice history, gondolas. She had them all.

Then she checked the list of handouts she would be using over the course of the tour. Daily itineraries, "How to Get the Most of the Tour", Italian phrases and how to pronounce them, maps of each city, Marcus Aurelius quotes on Stoicism, lists of restaurants and sites for each city, suggested restaurants and shopping for each stop, "Basics of Italian Wine", Roman history, the Renaissance, and Venice.

Satisfied that she had the handouts, she pulled out the guest list. She would review them and try to get a start on learning the names.

Like other Kastner Tours, the group was limited to 18 guests. This was much smaller than all of the other tour companies, even the other high-end ones. Keeping the size small allowed Kastner to stay at boutique hotels and to personalize each guest's experience. Kastner was not a mass-market tour company. They charged more than others, but they provided a much better experience. Kastner had the highest consumer ratings of any of the tour groups. So, more affluent vacationers chose them. They were worth the additional cost.

Before she could start, she heard her phone ping. A new text message. From Angelo. He texted instead of returning her call. And she had called him several days ago. He said that he was coming from Florence. He just finished a tour and would be in Sorrento later Sunday night. It felt very terse and business-like. There were no greetings, no looking-forward-to-working-with-you, no ... nothing. She let out a deep sigh, and reminded herself that she had to get along with her driver. The image of Luca's warnings came back to her mind.

She read down the Guest List. Kastner always listed the guests in the order in which the reservations were made.

    1. Marsha Wells, Aventura, Florida
    2. Monica Barnes, Aventura, Florida

3. Arjun Bakshi, Columbia, Maryland
4. Maya Bakshi, Columbia, Maryland
5. Rebecca Park, South Barrington, Illinois.
6. David Park, South Barrington, Illinois.
7. Charles Collins, Inverness, Illinois
8. Sharon Collins, Inverness, Illinois
9. Sharon Hines, Carmel, Indiana
10. Terry Hines, Carmel, Indiana
11. Victoria Moore, Kinsale, Wisconsin.
12. Mark Moore, Kinsale, Wisconsin.
13. Kecia Jackson, San Diego, California
14. James Jackson, San Diego, California
15. Susan Allen, Raleigh, North Carolina
16. Charlotte Johnson, Fuquay Varina, North Carolina
17. Lisa Carson, Brookhaven, Georgia
18. Brooke Jacoby, Hartford, Connecticut

With each tour, she tried to guess ahead of time what the people would be like. Most were probably wealthy, but there would probably be several who weren't. They had just saved their money for a European splurge. They were always the ones who were most excited about the tour and got the most pleasure out of the traveling. Richer Americans who traveled a lot could often be the fussier ones. Still, if the group fit the Kastner profile, they will be relatively well-off, in their 50s and 60s, with maybe a few sons or daughters. Maybe a couple of single travelers.

Mellow rehearsed the names, trying to remember the hometowns. After several minutes, she gave up and took a long, slow sip of her wine. Better, she thought, to wait until she would have faces to match up to the names. Right now, she would enjoy the Brunello.

Her thoughts wandered. Luca will do what he is going to do, all she can do is take responsibility for the tour. You can't control what happens to you; you can only control what you do about it. Things don't always happen like you want them to, you just have to work your way through them. And she would work through this challenge by making sure she pleased everyone; the guests, Angelo, the hotel staff, the local guides, and anyone else even remotely connected to the tour.

Chapter 4

Sorrento

Sunday, May 19, 2019

Mark

Mark Moore, with his mother Victoria beside him, walked into Olivia's View and took a quick scan of the gathering. The room was set up for a buffet dinner, with rounds of eight, a buffet line, and a dessert table. The potted lemon trees, with huge, bright yellow lemons, dominated the room. White tablecloths and flowered centerpieces, with tapered candles, also caught his eye. The silverware and glassware twinkled from the muted overhead chandeliers. Statues of ancient Romans lined the walls. He turned to Victoria. "Wow."

"I'll say. I think you picked the right tour." She shook her head slowly. "I have never seen real lemon trees before. These are amazing. The lemons are so big, and there are so many on each tree."

Mark saw the group, still assembling, mingling on the outdoor rooftop. He checked his watch. They were about ten minutes away from the scheduled 6:00 P.M start time. They made their way through the open glass doors, and Victoria immediately hustled over to the railing. She looked back at Mark and said, perhaps too loudly, "Oh my God! Would you look at this view?"

Mark saw that others were smiling at her expression. He joined her at the railing and said, "Mom, will you keep it down? You don't have to talk so loud."

"Yeah, sure. Well just look."

Mark first took in the Bay of Naples. The water was deep blue. And perfectly still; not a ripple. He looked at least 50 feet straight down. Olivia's View sat on a cliff overlooking the Bay. The orange ball of a sun was peeking through a scattering of dark gray clouds, only a few hours from setting on the Mediterranean. He looked across and saw the lights of Naples, curving to the right around the Bay. He looked to his right just as the clouds moved and Mt. Vesuvius took on the full force of direct sunlight. The brightness of the mountain stood in contrast to the dark blue of the Bay, and the busyness of the Naples shoreline. Spectacular. He did pick the right tour.

A server appeared beside them. "*Buona sera.* I am Anna. Can I get you something to drink?"

Victoria answered first, "I'll have a Diet Coke".

"Is a Coca-Cola Light OK?"

"Yeah, sure."

Anna shifted her gaze to Mark. "And you sir?"

"What kind of wine are you serving tonight?"

"What would you like? We have many, many choices."

"Well, I like hearty, full-bodied reds. Very dry."

"We have a Brunello. A 2011 Baricci. It is one of the favorites of Miss Melody, your Tour Director. Can I bring you a glass?"

"Oh, absolutely. And can you please put ice in her Coca-Cola?"

Anna replied, "Certainly, sir," and disappeared.

Mark was amazed that they were serving a Brunello. The king of Italian wines. Not a 2010, which was a vintage for the ages, but 2011 was a very good year for Brunello. Anna could not know, obviously, that Mark was a wine merchant. And Anna handled Victoria perfectly. He knew from his prior trips that Diet Coke is not available in Italy. The closest you could get is Coca-Cola Light. He had told his mother, a Diet Coke addict, that she would not be able to get it and that she would have to ask for Coca-Cola Light, which would have a very slightly different taste. He had also told her to ask for ice, as it was normally only provided in European restaurants if you specifically asked for it. Yet, here on the very first opportunity, she had forgotten both of these forewarnings. He figured that he had wasted his time with his other alerts about washcloths, asking for the check at a restaurant, not expecting Equal or Splenda packets, and Caffe Americano. Those were probably gone too. It should be an interesting trip. He would have to keep an eye on her.

Victoria pulled out her iPhone and took a picture. Then she began to talk with the two women next to them at the railing. Not surprising. He figured she would be everyone's friend by Tuesday. He listened in while he looked over the other guests.

"Yes, it's a spectacular view, isn't it?

"I am so looking forward to this trip."

Mark saw that he was probably the youngest of the group. The only other person who was even close was a very short woman with reddish-brown hair and wearing a pale blue scarf over a white top. No one seemed to be paired with her, so Mark assumed she was the Tour Director. The others were in small groups, looking like foursomes that were just meeting.

"We are from Kinsale, Wisconsin. I am here with my son. Mark, say hello to these two nice ladies."

"Of course. Very pleased to meet you".

"I always wanted to see Italy but could never get my late husband to take me. So, my wonderful son Mark is taking me on this Tour, even though he is a very busy executive. He is a wine expert for Liffey River Enterprises."

Mark put his hand on her arm, "Mom, stop already. They don't want to hear about all of that." He turned to the two women, "Where are you from?"

"Raleigh. I'm Susan. This is my sister Charlotte."

Charlotte picked up, "Call me Char. I'm from Fuquay Varina. It's a town just outside of Raleigh."

Mark shook their hands. "Very pleased to meet you both."

Anna appeared and delivered the drinks. Victoria gave a polite thank you and Mark said, *"Grazie"*, which generated a smile and a *"Prego"* from Anna as she left.

Victoria proceeded with Susan and Char. "My son is a very eligible bachelor, so if you have any daughters, nieces, or acquaintances that are looking, you will have to let me know."

"Mom. Please stop." He took a slow sip of his wine, and caught the two sisters exchange smiling glances. They were clearly amused by the doting mother they had just met.

"Well, I am just trying to be helpful." Victoria then followed with her distinctive hyena laugh. A hearty staccato, with just *too* much volume, and ending with a trailing sigh. Not *too* loud, just enough to call attention to herself.

Mark felt the eyes of the other guests looking over to see who was laughing. The sisters were smiling even more brightly.

He was rescued by the tinny sound of the Tour Director tapping a water glass to get everyone's attention.

He again noted her small size, seeing what looked like the tiny physique of an Olympic gymnast. Maybe five foot one, maybe 110 pounds. Looking more closely, her curves were more generous than most gymnasts. Her latte-colored hair hung just over the tops of her ears, and her bangs were well off her blue eyes. Or were they hazel?

She asked the group for their attention and began her remarks. *"Buona sera!* That's *good evening* in Italian. And welcome to Italy. My name is Melody O'Neal, but I go by Mellow. I am your guide and Tour Director. This tour is one of Kastner's most popular tours and, by the time we finish, I am sure that you will see why. Over the next ten days you will get to experience some spectacular scenery, some amazing food and wine, if, like me, wine is to your liking, and some of the most interesting history you will find anywhere on the planet. I will be providing a ton of information and handouts along the way. Now, after our reception dinner I will give some more details on the tour and how things will operate. But, first, I think you should all start to get to know each other. So, I'd like everyone to introduce themselves. Let's stick to name, where you are from, and one other thing about yourself. For this additional thing, I want you to tell us what your *passion* is. What are you really passionate about? The only rule is that you can't say that your passion is your children, grandchildren, or family. That's a given, so give us something else, like art, sports, travel, theatre, music, crafts, reading, or something like that. Who would like to go first?"

Victoria shot her hand up, "Oh, I can go first." She caught herself and pulled back, "Oh, is that alright? Can I go?"

"Of course."

"My name is Victoria Moore. I am from Kinsale, Wisconsin. My passion, oh it is so hard to narrow it down to one thing, but, if I had to, I would say that it is music. Especially classical. I am with my son here…" and she pointed to Mark.

Mark picked up, "And I am Mark Moore, also from Kinsale. My passion is wine and," raising his glass toward Mellow, "my compliments on the wine. It is terrific."

Mellow, addressing the entire group, followed with, "*Grazie*, that's Italian for *thank you*. Let's just go left to right for the next person." She looked at one of the North Carolina sisters.

Char went next, "My name is Charlotte Johnson. I go by Char. I am from Fuquay Varina, North Carolina, which is just outside of Raleigh. My passion is cooking. I love to have people over for dinner and prepare new dishes. I am traveling with my sister, who is right here." She pointed at Susan.

"And I am Susan Allen, from Raleigh. I would have to say that gardening is my passion."

The introductions continued, with people calling out their

passions in turn. Mark heard college basketball, orchids, U.S. history, poetry, and others until he couldn't keep track anymore.

Mark looked back at Mellow while some were talking. Her resting face was a cheerful smile, with a slight dimple on her left cheek.

Near the end, David Park said his passion was, "believe it or not, furniture design." Becca said David was her husband and her passion was interior design. Charles and Sharon Collins said that they were traveling with the Parks. His passion was baseball, while hers was yoga and mindfulness.

Once all were done, Mellow made motions to usher them into the dining area. But, Brooke Jacoby, from Hartford, asked Mellow, "So what is your passion?"

"Great question. I should declare as well, shouldn't I? It's travel and history. I am an American but I grew up in Germany. My father was with the U.S. Foreign Service in Berlin, and my mother was a translator at the embassy. They both made sure that I saw as much of Europe as I could. It created a love of travel that has stuck with me." She started toward the dining area.

Several took a last look at the view from the railing.

The North Carolina sisters joined Mark and Victoria at a table. Char and Susan were next to Victoria, and a gentleman asked if his group of four could join them. Mark noticed he favored his right leg while walking. He judged him to be late fifties, early sixties, but rather athletic looking for his age. He obviously worked out. Introductions followed. Next to Mark was David Park, the man with the slight limp, and his wife Becca, from South Barrington, Illinois and then Charles and Sharon Collins, from Inverness, Illinois. The two couples were traveling together. A foursome who looked to all be in the same age range. Well, not exactly. Becca seemed a bit younger. Mark noticed that her eyes darted from person to person.

Small talk ensued, with Victoria, of course, leading the way. Victoria asked David Park, "Are you the David Park that owns all of the furniture stores in the Chicago area?"

"Yes, I am. We have 11 stores in all."

"I thought I recognized you. Well, I just love your commercials. I have seen you in them. And I have been in your stores. They are terrific."

"Thank you." He pointed politely toward Charles, "Charles here heads up my store operations."

Charles nodded, and Becca chimed in, "We also have another part of the business that focuses on antiques and architectural salvage. Have you heard of *Architectural Treasures by David Park*?"

Victoria's reply of, "No, sorry I haven't" produced an instant frown on Becca's face.

Mellow appeared and directed them to the buffet.

The options added up to a remarkable feast. Crostini with chicken liver pate. Zucchini flowers with parmesan mashed potatoes. Parma ham with asparagus and peas. Ravioli with ricotta and cherry tomatoes. Lemon risotto with lobster and pesto. Grouper with saffron and lime. Beef fillet with potato croquet.

It was overwhelming, and a good part of the dinner conversation consisted of exclamations about how amazing everything tasted. When Mellow arrived to tell them that the dessert table was now open, they all gave a feigning "No I can't, I'm too full," but then proceeded to the table anyway. Tiramisu, cannoli, sponge biscuits with dark chocolate mousse, and several enticing flavors of gelato. All house-made.

Over his gelato, Mark heard David quietly ask Becca for "my pill".

Becca replied, also softly, "Honey, you already took it. A couple of hours ago."

"No, I didn't." David was louder, and everyone at the table glanced over. Mark took a sip of his wine and exchanged glances with his mother.

"I'll show you." Becca pulled an all-week pill case from her purse and opened up the compartment marked *S* for Sunday. She showed it to David, "See, one left. That's for tonight. You took your dinner one early."

David, even louder now, protested. "Can't you just give me my damn pill?"

Mark now saw that people from the other tables were looking over to see what the conflict was. It was all very awkward.

Mellow appeared, from nowhere it seemed to Mark. "Can I help with anything here?"

Becca replied, "No, we are fine. I just need to give David his pill." She poured the remaining pill onto David's plate. He took it, said nothing, and then went back to his tiramisu.

Mark was anxious to move on, and he turned to Mellow. "I have to compliment you on the wine. I did not expect to get a Brunello tonight. It is a fabulous wine."

"Thank you. It's one of my favorites."

Victoria joined the conversation, "Well you two seem to have something in common." She looked at Mellow, "Mark here is a wine expert."

Mark groaned inside. He tried to head her off, "Well I don't claim to be an expert. I am just a wine buyer back in Wisconsin."

"Oh, he is being too modest. He is the top wine merchant for Liffey River Enterprises. That's one of the largest distributors in the country."

Mark caught the North Carolina sisters again smiling at each other.

But Mellow handled it well. She looked at Mark and said, "Well that is certainly impressive. I look forward to hearing what you think about the wines you have on the tour. Now, please excuse me. I need to talk to the group about tomorrow." And she was off.

Mellow called for the group's attention and made a few announcements. Tomorrow they would drive the Amalfi Coast. They were in luck that the weather was expected to be clear and sunny. The views should be terrific. She explained the seating on the coach. Seats would be assigned, so there is no need to try to rush to the coach to get a good seat. They would rotate seating each day, in a clockwise direction.

She handed out a guest list, showing names and hometowns. Next came several pages of a detailed itinerary, complete with hotel names, stops, meals, sites, start times, and ending times. Then, she reviewed some suggestions for getting the most out of the tour, and they all made perfect sense to Mark. Stay flexible. Some things might go wrong, go with the flow. Talk with the locals a lot, Italians are wonderful people and interacting with them will make for a richer experience. We are in a group, but we are not a herd. There is plenty of free time for them to explore each location on their own.

She closed with, "Above all else, please stay alert to changes in the schedule. It is very likely that, for any number of reasons, our times for events will have to be adjusted. So please stay alert. I will make announcements as things change. And, you see from the detailed itinerary that the buffet breakfast tomorrow starts at 6:30. We will meet at the coach at 7:30. It's an early start tomorrow."

She paused momentarily. "And now there is one final topic I want to mention, and I almost hesitate to bring it up. On some of our Kastner tours over the past couple of years there have been some of what I will call *spirited discussions* about politics back in the U.S. These have impacted the enjoyment that our guests have had on some of our tours. I know that things are getting pretty polarized back there. So, with your permission, I would like to declare this entire tour a *politics-free* zone. Can I get a thumbs up from those would like that?"

Mark saw that, within seconds, half the hands gave a thumbs up. Some said, "Here, here!" The rest of the hands followed suit, his included. Thank God!

As the dinner ended, Mark noticed that David and Becca left immediately. They had not said a word to each other, or anyone else, since the outburst. He figured that they would continue the argument back in their hotel room.

Mark and Victoria said goodbye to the sisters, and Victoria said she wanted to ask Mellow a question. She started toward her, and

Mark followed.

Mellow was already talking with other guests, so they waited a couple of minutes. As Mellow freed up, she turned to Victoria. "*Buona sera.*"

"Hi, I just want to tell you how much I am looking forward to this trip. I just have a question about shopping."

"Sure."

"Will you be telling us the best places to buy things at? I expect to buy a lot on this trip and you obviously know more than I do about shopping in Italy."

"Certainly. I have handouts for shopping and restaurants in Sorrento, Rome, Florence, and Venice. Are you looking for anything in particular?"

"Well, I heard that Sorrento is a good place for inlaid wood. I am looking for a small table for a very specific spot in my dining room."

Mark noticed that Becca walked up beside them. She was tall and somewhat heavy. She walked with the moves of a graceful athlete, and Mark envisioned her as a former volleyball spiker who had only just recently let herself start to go. As before, her eyes seemed to flicker around her, as if always monitoring who might be watching.

He looked, but did not see David. He thought Becca was a bit too close. Mellow herself looked at her and nodded.

Mellow replied to Victoria, "Sorrento is the best place for inlaid wood. Tomorrow I will give you some specific shops you might try."

Mark, with Becca so close to the trio, figured the only polite thing to do would be to pull Becca into the conversation. "We are talking about shopping, my mother's favorite topic. Do you want to join us?"

"Oh, thank you. That's OK. I don't mean to interrupt. I just want to apologize about David. He's not himself just now."

"That's quite alright," Mellow said.

"He has been diagnosed with early Alzheimer's. He forgets things, and can get confused. Then he gets frustrated and loses his temper. He *did* take his pill before we came down for the reception."

Becca stopped and shook her head slowly. Mark thought she looked to be on the verge of tears.

Mellow said, "I am so sorry Becca. Thank you for letting me know. I hope you are taking care of yourself. Being a caregiver can be stressful."

"It doesn't help that he just had knee surgery. He fell when he was riding his bike in our forest preserve. That was about five weeks ago. The doctor prescribed these pain pills." She held up the amber, plastic prescription bottle. "The doctor said they are really strong, so he has to be careful with how many he takes. Especially with his memory and forgetting things. That's why I put them in this day-of-the-week container. I have to watch that he doesn't take too many." Her eyes were still very glassy.

Mellow replied, "Well, he is lucky to have you to watch for things."

"I think the knee hurts worse than he lets on. We probably shouldn't have even done this trip. But David was insistent. He is a wonderful man, but he can be really bullheaded about things."

Mellow answered, "If there is anything you need from me during this trip, please just let me know."

Victoria added, "I am so sorry to hear this. If Mark or I can help, we will be happy to do so, as well."

Becca thanked them both, wiped her nose with a tissue that seemed to appear from nowhere, and walked off.

Chapter 5

Amalfi

Monday, May 20, 2019

Mellow

Mellow wheeled her supply box through the front doors of The Olivian and headed toward the coach. Angelo was standing by the open door of the coach. He was probably in his early fifties, stocky and compact. A balding head and a graying mustache projected the image of a craggy, older bouncer at a tough Italian bar.

She let out a long, slow breath as she approached.

She put out her hand and, with a generous smile, said, "*Buongiorno*, Angelo. I'm Melody. You can call me Mellow. Everyone does."

He took her hand and gave her a feeble "*Buongiorno*". He dropped her hand and folded his arms across his chest. His eyes stayed on her and Mellow felt a piercing eye contact.

"Well, I am looking forward to working with you." She tried to be cheerful. "I think we have a good group for the tour. They seemed to have a lot of energy at last night's dinner."

Angelo looked at his watch. "We only have about 30 minutes before they start to get here. So, let me just say what I want to say. I made some calls when I found out you would be the Tour Director. Everyone said that you were difficult to work with, you complain a lot, and you try to tell everyone how to do their jobs. Let me be clear. You are in charge of the tour, but I am in charge of the coach. As long as you understand that, we will get along. If not, you and I will have big problems." He paused before he continued, "And one other thing. No jokes about my name. I have heard them all and they are old. And not funny."

Mellow eyed him, her mind racing on how to handle this guy. The old Mellow would have said: *Listen Pal. You may look like a tough guy who can handle himself, but just drop the attitude. You have no call to be so hostile. You and I have to work together for the next ten days. The only time I get after people is when they don't do their job, and it affects the guests. And if you don't do what you should, I will get all over you too. So just lose the attitude.*

But, the shadow of Luca's warnings—"not a single complaint, nothing can go wrong"—caused her to become the new Mellow, the I-have-to-save-my-job Mellow. She dropped her eyes, uttered a meek "I understand", and walked past him onto the coach.

The coach was a custom McGregor. The outside was white with muted blue trim. Unlike other tour companies, Kastner did not plaster their name all over the outside. The only lettering consisted of the Kastner name in a smallish font on each side of the coach. That way the guests could find the coach, without having it shout "here come the tourists" throughout Europe. Tall, smoky glass allowed the guests great views from the inside. The coach had 12 rows of seats, overhead storage, a PA system, drop-down video monitors for every other row, power ports for plug-in devices, a wifi system, a mid-sized refrigerator in the front, and a restroom in the back. The effect was that the vehicle was more of a large and elegant limousine, instead of a small and fancy bus, which was the exact feel that Kastner was looking for. It was roomy, but still small enough to navigate the twists and turns of the Amalfi drive.

Mellow got her box of supplies ready, and put up the guest names over their assigned rows. She would move these each day to indicate the clockwise rotation for each day. Then she put personalized folders on each seat, with the Monday handouts inside. She checked to see if Angelo was looking. He wasn't, so she walked to the back to check the restroom. It was spotless, as clean as she had ever seen on a Kastner coach. That was a relief.

Walking back to the front, she did a final check of the interior. She saw that a small crowd was forming outside the bus. She stepped out, posted the daily seating chart on the inside of the open door, and began to welcome the guests. Angelo stood beside her, positioned to help if any guests needed assistance with the first step.

Mellow was pleased with the buzz of conversation. Even among those who had just met the prior evening. She introduced each of them to Angelo. As they offered their names to him, she then pointed out their assigned row on the coach. It provided the practice needed to learn their names.

Once all were settled onboard, she took to the PA and began. "*Buongiorno.*"

She heard a smattering of "Good Mornings".

"Now we have to do better than that. You are in Italy, so I am going to make sure you learn at least a little Italian over the next ten days. *Buongiorno* means "good morning." So, when I say *buongiorno*, you say it back to me. *Buongiorno.*"

She heard a loud chorus back at her. Several laughed out loud.

"Excellent. Now, I want each of you to turn to someone sitting across from you, or in front of you or behind you and welcome them with a hearty *Buongiorno.*

Her request brought the coach to life, and several began to talk even beyond the greeting.

Once they quieted, she introduced Angelo again, as the driver who would navigate Italy for them for the next ten days. Then, it was on to the folders and the Monday handouts.

The first was a single sheet of English-Italian phrases. They practiced *buongiorno*, *buona sera*, *si*, and *no*. Badly, she thought. But she assured them that even trying to speak some Italian words or phrases would go a long way with the Italians they would meet. Tomorrow, she said, they would work on a few more.

The second handout was a map of the Sorrento peninsula, with highlights for Sorrento, Positano, Amalfi, Ravello, and Pompeii. "More about that as we get closer to our first stop at Positano," she said.

Third, a detailed street map of Sorrento, with callouts for The Olivian, recommended restaurants and cafes, and suggested shopping stops.

Mellow nodded to Angelo, and they started off to the Amalfi Coast. As they worked their way through Sorrento, Mellow went back to the PA system.

"Oh, one other thing. Several people asked about my blue scarf yesterday. Scarves are very popular in Italy. That was a silk one that I bought in Florence several years ago. Today I have this greenish one on. You will see a lot of women wearing scarves. Italians see them as a perfect accent to whatever you wear. They can dress up almost anything, and they can be a lifesaver when you want to look casual but fashionable. I had a woman on a tour a few years ago who said, 'Yeah, and they cover up my turkey neck!' But I don't think anyone in this group has that problem."

The open laughter, including Victoria saying "Yeah, sure", signaled the desirable energy of the group.

Victoria raised her hand, and Mellow called on her. "I noticed that your scarf is tied very loosely. Don't you knot it?"

"Oh no! The thought of anything tight around my neck just gives me the creeps. I know it's ridiculous, but I would feel like I am being strangled if it is knotted up and tight."

She waited for any other questions, then went on. "Our first stop will be a small town called Positano. We will take a short stretch break, and then continue on to Amalfi. We will stop in Amalfi for about an hour and a half, and then continue on to Ravello, which is a resort village up in the mountains. Our lunch will be in a delightful café that overlooks the water. It is almost looking down directly at Amalfi. The view is wonderful. Then, we will head back to The Olivian and get you back in time for several hours of free time in Sorrento. We should be back by three o'clock or so. And, just a reminder, dinner is on your own tonight. I left a list of suggested restaurants in your folder."

Mellow looked down the rows. Almost all were looking out the window to take in the town. She expected that. They came to look at Italy, not her. So, she went on to her explanation of Amalfi History. They could listen while they looked.

"Amalfi was once one of the major maritime powers for the Mediterranean. Back in the eleventh and twelfth centuries, they competed with Pisa and Genoa for control of the trade in the Mediterranean." She went on, but she didn't get very far.

Instead, Angelo turned the coach onto the road to Positano, and the coast came into view. The water reflected a mix of multiple shades of blue. Streaks of azure, turquoise nearer the shore, deep cobalt farther out, splashes of periwinkle along the whole stretch. All shimmering softly from the mild breeze and morning angle of the sun.

Mellow was interrupted by "Oh's", "Wow's", and "Oh-my-god's" from the rows of guests. She knew it was useless to try to compete with the views of the water. No one was listening to her. So, she told them she would continue with the Amalfi history later in the drive. Even though she had seen the coast dozens of times, she was also taken with the display of color. She turned off the PA and sat back to enjoy the drive.

The time to Positano was longer than expected. Even with their early departure the road was jammed with cars, scooters, motorcycles, buses, and even hikers. With virtually no shoulder, every vehicle inched along. And even though they had all probably heard about the drive, she heard the guests talking about how amazed they were at the narrowness, the zig-zags, the curves, the switchbacks, the steep inclines, the rapid descents, and the stop-and-go. All with sheer 100-foot to 300-foot drop-offs just a few feet from the tires of the coach. Mellow smiled inside because she knew that the next leg of the drive, from Positano to Amalfi, 12 miles further, was even more amazing.

As they approached Positano, she came back on the PA. "We are a little behind, so I want to keep our stop for about 20 minutes. We will have a longer stop in Amalfi. This stop is just to give you a chance to stretch your legs, take a few pictures, and use the restrooms if you need to. A word about the restrooms. Italy has public restrooms that charge a fee. It is usually one euro. You put the coin in the slot and push your way through the turnstile. Not everyone will have coins handy, so I have put a small basket up front here with several coins." She held up the basket for all to see.

"If you need one, go ahead and take one. Now, some of the restrooms are for men, and some are for women. So, I will call them *Summer Rooms* during our tour. Some are for men and some are for women." She paused and got the chuckles she was after.

"Each time we stop, I will point out where the Summer Rooms are located. In Positano, they will be about half of a block further down the road, on the opposite side. Also, I have a larger basket up front with bottled water, if you want to take one."

Angelo pulled the coach into a parking slot, opened the door, and stepped off. He then stood ready to offer his hand to anyone needing assistance.

As Mellow stepped down, she said, "Thank you, Angelo. That was excellent driving."

He nodded and offered a mild, "*Grazie*".

Several guests took the coins and started toward the Summer Rooms. Only a few took the chilled water.

Victoria and Mark stood near the coach and took in the view of the beach. Most of the guests stayed near the coach and started to take photos of the shore and the town.

Victoria asked Mellow if she would take a picture of her and her son Mark. Mellow obliged. As she handed the iPhone back, Victoria said, "I want to get your picture too. Mark, stand next to Mellow. I want to get a shot of you two, with the town in the background."

Mark and Mellow walked several steps from the bus, put their backs to the town, and smiled for the photo.

Victoria snapped several in succession. "Perfect!"

Mellow noticed that David Park was still on the coach. His wife Becca, along with their friends, Sharon and Charles Collins, were walking along the road, gawking at the shoreline and the buildings of Positano. So Mellow went back on the coach to check on David.

"How are we doing in here?"

"Oh, I'm fine. It's just that with this knee it doesn't seem worth it to get off the bus if it's only going to be a few minutes. It is still pretty sore. And stiff."

"Well, you know best. Just let me know if I can do anything, alright."

"Thank you."

With everyone adhering to the time limit for the stop, they soon continued on their way to Amalfi. The road from Positano to Amalfi was just as harrowing, maybe even more so. And the views were even more spectacular.

Sharon and Charles Collins were only a few rows behind Mellow and she heard them talking. Sharon said she was getting a little woozy and nauseated from the constant turns of the coach. So, Mellow walked back to talk with them.

"How are we doing here?"

Sharon said, "Not so good. I am getting dizzy from all of the turns."

Susan and Char, the sisters from North Carolina, were sitting in the row in front of them. Susan turned back and said, "I have ginger tablets. They're chewable."

Charles asked, "What do those do?"

"They help with nausea."

Char joined in, "Susan is a pharmacist in Raleigh. And a pretty good one."

Susan went on, "Ginger is naturally occurring, and is perfectly safe. You do not need a prescription."

Mellow could see that Sharon was considering it.

She asked Mellow, "What do you think? Should I try it?"

"That is completely up to you. I can't offer any kind of medical advice or any medications, prescription or otherwise. It is against Kastner policy. A liability issue for the company."

Sharon turned back to Becca, who was sitting just behind her. "What do you think?"

Becca said, "I think she is a pharmacist and probably knows what she is talking about. Besides, it can't hurt."

Sharon nodded and asked Pharmacist Susan for a ginger tablet. Susan obliged, and Sharon thanked her for offering.

Mellow said, "Let me know how you are feeling. I hope it works for you."

As Mellow walked back to her seat, she overheard the sisters talking with Sharon and Charles. She learned that Susan was a pharmacist at a CVS in Raleigh. Her sister Char was a Walgreen's Store Manager in nearby Fuquay Varina.

While on route, Angelo brought the coach to a full stop right on the road. Mellow looked ahead and saw that Angelo had stopped about five car lengths behind the car ahead of them. Sure enough, a bus was coming from the opposite direction and the car had to back up so the bus could make the sharp turn. Angelo had seen this coming and stopped far enough behind that he did not have to back up as well. The curves ahead, including a stone bridge over a steep ravine, were visible.

She heard the guest behind her, Arjun Bakshi, from Columbia, Maryland, say, "Oh my god, look at that. It looks like the road we are going to go over is just hanging over a cliff."

Mellow turned her head back and said, "It is a pretty amazing drive, isn't it?"

After another steep rise, and then a descent, they approached

Amalfi. The town looked like pastel building blocks stacked on top of each other, with a sprinkling of stone and greenery. And the sun was higher in the sky, casting the town in bright sunlight. Mellow took to the PA.

"We will be stopping for about an hour and a half. You have plenty of time to walk through the town. It is not that big, but the streets are very narrow and winding. You will find some terrific shops, boutiques, and cafes. I recommend that you find your way to the Cathedral of St. Andrew. The oldest part of the complex goes back to the sixth century. You go about one block north up the main road and it will be on your right. It is well worth the visit. One caution, the steps are very old and very uneven. There are no handrails, so you have to really watch your step."

She checked the refrigerator and saw that Angelo had restocked it with bottled water during the Positano stop.

"We have waters available if anyone would like one. And, the Summer Rooms are going to be up the main street, on your left."

She checked her watch. "Let's meet back here at the coach at 11:00."

The guests left the coach, and Mellow noticed that David waited until all were off before he started to leave the coach. Becca waited with him, and they were joined by Sharon and Charles once David was off the coach. David was clearly laboring to walk, so Angelo helped him off the steps. Mellow went over to the foursome as they discussed their plans.

David said, "I think I will just sit here on one of these benches. You all go ahead. I will be fine."

Sharon turned to Charles and said, "Honey, why don't you two just go ahead. I am still a bit woozy and think I will sit this one out, as well. I am still moving side to side." Becca and Charles each offered to stay with their spouses, but both David and Sharon insisted that they go ahead and walk through Amalfi.

Thirty minutes later, Mellow walked into the Moretti Bakery. Mama Moretti hustled around the counter to greet her. "Oh, Miss

Mellow, Miss Mellow."

She grabbed Mellow into a full-on hug, and Mellow returned the embrace. The two exchanged the cheek-touching you expect from close friends that have not seen each other for a while.

"I am so glad that you called, and so happy that are stopping in."

"Well, I couldn't very well come to Amalfi and not stop in to see the best baker in all of Italy, could I?"

Mama Moretti let out a hearty laugh, and waved her away, "Oh, stop it."

"Come back in the kitchen here. I have your *sfogliatella*. Three dozen, just like you asked. I was so excited to get your call. Does this mean that you are going to be coming here again? We certainly missed you."

Mellow followed her into the kitchen and found herself smiling broadly. Mama still had all of her energy and exuberance for life. "I am not sure, Mama. We will have to see."

Mama stopped just inside the kitchen door and turned, "So, tell me. Is there a man yet?"

"Not yet, Mama. It is hard to meet men in the job I have."

"Well, we have a woman here in the village who is just fantastic at finding husbands for women. And wives for men. You let me know if you want to talk with her."

"I will do that, Mama."

Mama moved three boxes across the table and opened them for Mellow's inspection. "Here you go. Three different types. Small ones, just like you ordered. Ricotta, almond paste, and whipped cream."

Mellow looked down at the pastries. *Sfogliatella* is a clam-shaped pastry with the flaky texture of a croissant. Ricotta was the traditional filling. Mama must have seen the disappointment in Mellow's face because she quickly let out another laugh and pushed a fourth box over. "And here are six chocolate ones, just for you. Don't share them with the Americans. I made them just for you because I know that you love your chocolate."

"These are all perfect." She knew the guests would love them, especially when she told them the story of how they were originally created 400 years ago in a monastery a few miles down the coast. She knew that at least a few of the guests might recognize them as *lobster tails*, the American version of the pastry.

Mellow paid her, in cash of course, and visited a bit longer. Then, she gathered up the boxes and started toward the front door.

Mama stopped her. "No, no, no, Mellow. You are family, you can go out this door right here. Did you forget?" She pointed toward a door that opened up to the alley. Mellow had used it many times before and knew it was a shortcut, only two quick turns, back to the main street of Amalfi.

"Of course, Mama. Now you take care of yourself, alright? *Ciao!*"

They again exchanged hugs and air kisses. Then Mellow started toward the door.

As she was about to open it, she saw that a couple, looked like an older couple, were in a passionate embrace, leaning against the stone wall in the alley. She smiled to herself, as they continued their kissing. The woman's hand was exploring the man's back, rubbing sensuously, and Mellow could tell that he, in turn, was massaging the woman's back. Maybe even lower. Mellow figured she would wait a few seconds for them to separate before heading out. But they showed no signs of letting up.

So, Mellow pushed the door open and stepped out. The noise of the door, along with her footsteps, broke the embrace.

As they turned toward the noise, Mellow found herself looking at Becca and Charles. The two who left their spouses back at the coach.

Becca's eyes locked on Mellow's, and her face went perfectly still.

Chapter 6

Amalfi

Monday, May 20, 2019

Mark

Mark left his mother in the gift shop and walked next door to the café. A server, Sylvia, took his order for a Café Americano. He pulled out the zip lock bag of Equal packets, courtesy of Mellow, and stirred then into his cup. Mellow had cleverly created small bags of 10 packets each of Equal and Splenda. Mark spotted them on his way out of the coach and asked about them. She said that she planned to explain about Equal and Splenda when they stopped for lunch, but that he was free to take one now if he wanted. She would make them available at the front of the coach. Smart. The woman seems like the type that thinks of everything. He knew from his prior trips that they would likely only find Sweet'N Low, the red packets of saccharin, in Italy. Somehow, she had gotten her hands on a lot of Equal and Splenda. He preferred Equal, as he felt like the aspartame had less of an aftertaste than the saccharin of Sweet'N Low.

He pulled out his iPhone and checked his emails. Nothing new.

He really didn't expect any, since they were seven hours ahead of Wisconsin. Back home, no one would be at work yet. Still, he was anxious to see if his boss had any news, or if he had gotten any business emails. He was expecting an important one. He hadn't gotten it when he checked before breakfast. He thought that maybe it was waiting to be released from some kind of queue in some server back in the U.S. Or, was it just force of habit because of his anxiety over the email? He checked his text messages. Nothing.

He knew others would criticize his constant checking of emails and voicemails. He was on vacation. He was supposed to *get away*. Leave the stress of work behind and relax. Forget about work for a while.

Hah! They just didn't understand. He would be even more anxious if he didn't check emails and voicemails. He would fret and worry that something was happening and he didn't know about it. Strangely perhaps, he was more relaxed if he checked his email and messages and then knew that there wasn't anything to worry about. And if something was wrong, then at least he would know about it and could address it. It was the *not knowing* that put him on edge.

So, each night when he was on vacation, he would work through all of his emails and voice mails. Others would see that as stress-inducing. He saw it as stress-reducing.

Stress-inducing would be being away from the office for a week, not knowing what is going on, and then returning to a completely full inbox of emails and voicemails. That would drive him crazy.

No, they just didn't understand. Especially his mother. Hence, he snuck a peek into his phone whenever he could step away from her.

And they didn't know that he had an uncanny ability to shift his attention and focus almost immediately. He could write a detailed business email on his iPhone, hit send, and then instantly look out of the coach window and fully appreciate something like the marvel of the Amalfi Coast.

Satisfied that he wasn't missing anything, he put his iPhone away and took a long sip of his coffee. He watched the tourists go by. All sizes. All shapes. All ages.

He decided to play the "Spot the American" game. Last year in Florence, he was at an outdoor café with his Italian business counterparts and they introduced him to the game. They would sit at the table and see who could spot the most Americans. With some practice and feedback, he got pretty good at it. They taught him what to look for.

Baseball caps. Loud talking. Shirts with team logos. Cargo pants. Carrying a cup of coffee.

"On the positive side," his colleague Tommaso said, "they have very nice teeth compared to almost anyone in Europe. Straight and white. If I meet someone with white teeth that aren't crooked, I know right away that they are American."

Christian had added, "And they smile more. I think Europeans are trained from birth to keep this disinterested, blank look on their face. Americans always seem to be happy and cheerful."

Other signs that they had agreed upon? Taking pictures. White tennis shoes. Overweight, with loose-fitting clothes. And backpacks were a dead give-away.

Mark was up to 23 when Victoria finally rejoined him. He wanted to count her as number 24, but figured that would be cheating.

Chapter 7

Amalfi

Monday, May 20, 2019

Mellow

Mellow maintained her eye contact while Becca continued her frozen stare. After several seconds, Becca glanced quickly at Charles, and then back to Mellow. She shook her head slowly, and started to talk, "I can ex—"

Mellow shot her hand up in a sign of *stop*, "I don't want to hear or know about this. When it comes to … consenting adults, I am a complete libertarian." Privately, she was disgusted. Their spouses were back at a bench by the coach, one trying her best not to vomit, and the other struggling to walk after his knee surgery. And these two go off canoodling, having their affair. Or whatever this is.

Charles was red-faced and staring down at the stone pavement. Becca spoke up, and Mellow saw a flare of anger in Becca's eyes, "You can't say anything. This is none of your business. You have to keep quiet and act like you never saw us."

Charles followed with pleading eyes, "Please."

"You are right. This is not my business. This is all between you two and your spouses." She then imagined the spouses discovering the affair and Becca blaming her about it. She imagined Becca or Charles calling Kastner tours and complaining. Lucca would be furious, and she would then definitely get fired.

Mellow closed off the interaction. "The only thing I ask is that you don't do anything that disrupts the tour."

Becca gave a resigned, "We won't", and Mellow started back to the coach.

Once they were en route to Ravello, Mellow announced the treat she had, and she walked the aisle, handing out napkins and allowing each guest to select one of the *sfogliatella*. She did her best to avoid eye contact with Becca and Charles. She wondered what was really going on. How long? Do their spouses suspect?

When she returned to the PA system, she explained the origin of the pastry and described Mama Moretti's bakery. A revered Amalfi establishment.

She walked up by Angelo and said, "I know you can't have one while you are driving, so I will leave them right here on this seat. Once we stop, take as many of whatever flavor you like."

Angelo turned to her in surprise. "*Grazie*. That is very kind of you." He turned back to the road, "Most tour directors don't do this kind of thing, buy treats for the guests. And certainly not for the drivers."

"*Prego*. It's my pleasure."

Mellow settled back into her seat. Now would be a good time to remind Angelo to gas up and wash the coach once they got back to Sorrento. Well, maybe not *remind* him. Maybe just *suggest* it. Or, better yet, ask him where he plans to buy the gas and wash the coach back in Sorrento. Act like she was just curious. No, that would be too obvious. The Old Mellow would have just blurted out the reminder. But get-along-with-everyone Mellow suppressed herself. She was trying to trust. But, oh, it was hard. So, so hard.

A guest, James Jackson, raised his hand and asked, "Aren't we near Salerno? Wasn't there a big beach landing there, or some kind of big battle in World War II?"

She picked up the microphone and started to tell the guests about the Allied landing at Salerno in World War II. It was just 15 miles down the coast. "Imagine this," she said, "It's 1943, the Allied forces have 500 ships in the Bay of Salerno, and they have about 180,000 to 200,000 troops. The Germans and Italians number about 125,000." She continued to explain that it was a very nasty affair and neither side accomplished their objectives. But the Allies established a foothold in Italy and proceeded to march north through Italy. She told them that she remembered her father taking her to the Museum in Salerno, where she saw photos, videos, uniforms, and weapons used in the battle.

Chapter 8

Sorrento

Monday, May 20, 2019

Becca

Becca gave David the aisle seat for the return drive to Sorrento. His head was back, and his eyes were mostly closed. Lunch proved to be another amazing feast. Coupled with the breathtaking views of the Bay of Salerno, with Amalfi in the foreground, all of the guests were celebrating the day. Becca heard a continual buzz of conversation. The coach had the inside lane for the drive back, so the group was spared the cliff-hanging turns. Instead of the cliffs being three or five feet from the tires, they were now a full fifteen feet away. Compared to the morning drive, it was a relief.

David had struggled with the walk from the coach to the restaurant, as the path was steep and several blocks long. During lunch he took two of his painkillers instead of one. And after lunch, he had insisted on taking the paths to the overlooks. He was the last one to the restaurant, the last one to the lookouts, and the last one back to the coach. Now, the double dose was taking effect and even the noise of the conversations didn't keep him awake.

It gave Becca time to think. And she needed it. Right after Mellow had discovered her and Charles in the alley, she had gone into a mild panic. No, not mild. Full on panic. She should have known that their busybody Tour Director would be snooping around the town. It was Charles' idea to sneak off into an alley. He lamented that it had been almost ten days since they had had any kind of rendezvous, and he said it was "killing him." So, she went along. She had looked and not spotted any security cameras in the alleyway. Now, her whole plan was in jeopardy.

Mellow said she wouldn't say anything. But could she be trusted? She might talk about it anyway. She was talking with Angelo when David and Becca got back to the coach, and she was looking right at Becca when she kept on talking. What was she saying? Was she gossiping about Becca and Charles?

Mellow came over the PA system. Blabbering about questions she got over lunch. "Yes, a regular coffee in Italy means a very small cup of Expresso. If you want coffee like they have in the U.S., you have to ask for a Café Americano."

Regardless of what Mellow said about not saying anything, Becca would have to keep her distance from Charles. They had been caught. For the first time. All of those meetups back home, and here, five thousand miles away, they get caught.

"But Café Americano is not coffee like it is brewed in the U.S. It is actually an Italian expresso that is diluted with hot water."

Charles and Sharon were in the row ahead of Becca. She looked at the back of Charles' head and felt like giving it a smack. *You fool! Couldn't control yourself for a few more days.*

With time to think, the reality struck Becca. Once David dies from the opioid overdose the authorities will no doubt ask questions. And one of the first people they will talk to is Mellow. She's the Tour Director. They will ask if anything out of the ordinary happened. She will tell them about David snapping at me at the dinner at Olivia's View. And me telling her about the Alzheimer's and his pain pills. That would be OK. But then she will tell them about seeing me and Charles. And then they will get suspicious and ask a lot of questions.

She had to get Mellow off the tour. She couldn't have her around when David goes. But how? Could she call Kastner Tours and complain about her? No, she is obviously very good at what she does, and they wouldn't want to replace her. No, she would have to come up with another way to get rid of her, and to do it before she rids herself of David.

They were approaching The Olivian, and Mellow came back on the PA. "A couple of reminders before we separate for the day. Dinner tonight is on your own. I left a sheet in your folder with the names of some restaurants you might want to try. Most are at or near the *Piazza Tasso*, which is the main *piazza* in the center of town."

"Tomorrow we go to Pompeii and then on to Rome. Breakfast is available at 6:30, and our baggage pull will be at 6:45. Have your bags packed and in your rooms, just inside the door, before you go down for breakfast. Be sure that you have the Kastner Tour tags on them. We will have them picked up and put on the coach. We will plan on an 8:00 departure."

Then she looked at Victoria and Mark. "Victoria, see me when you get off the coach. I have a recommendation on where you can look for the inlaid wood furniture."

Chapter 9

Sorrento

Monday, May 20, 2019

Mark

Mark and Victoria had just settled on the table she would buy. He checked his watch. "Mom," he said, "it's 6:30, about time to find the restaurant for dinner. Why don't we wrap this up and find our way back to the Square? That's where the restaurant is at, the one Mellow recommended."

"Yeah, sure. It's called a *piazza*, you know."

"Oh, listen to you. Trying to talk like a local."

She looked over the table one last time, delighted with her choice. "This will be perfect! And the corner of my dining room will be the perfect place for it."

Mark inspected it again. It was inlaid with ten different colors and shades; it depicted wine glasses, a wine bottle, and several bunches of grapes. The colors were perfectly coordinated. Two small wheels on one end meant that it could be used as a serving cart. A hand-made work of art.

Anthony, one of the sons of Marino & Sons, wrote up the invoice and scanned Mark's Mastercard. The table would arrive in a few weeks. Tony himself would see to it. He would send Mark regular emails about the progress of the packing and shipping. "Anything for one of Miss Mellow's friends."

Mark and Victoria discovered that Mellow's name worked wonders at Marino & Sons. Mellow had explained that there were no fees or referral payments, as those were against Kastner policy. But, using Mellow's name resulted in a 30% discount and complimentary shipping. Mr. Marino himself had come out to look for Mellow once he heard that one of her friends was in the shop. Not finding her, he still insisted that Mark and Victoria come with him to the workshop in the back, for a personal tour. There they found Giovanni, the actual artist who made the table that they ended up buying, intent at a workbench, reconstructing the tiny pieces that would make up a colorful tabletop. Giovanni showed them, too quickly for Mark's preference, how he drew a design, stacked the paper-thin veneers, cut out the wood, and then re-assembled the pieces to make up the finished inlaid wood. Then, press it for several weeks and finish it off with polyurethane. The explanation was too fast for Mark's taste, as he was fascinated and wanted to see each step in detail. Giovanni was working on twelve layers of different colored veneers, painstakingly placing them in the correct position for what looked like a brain-exploding jigsaw puzzle. Amazing artistry and patience. Earlier, Giovanni himself was in the showroom and showed them the wine-themed table. He had turned the table over to show where he had engraved his personal signature. That had closed the sale with Victoria.

Mark again told himself that they had picked the right Tour group.

He opened the door for Victoria and led her out to the street. "I think we lucked out with having Mellow as our Tour Director." They started toward the restaurant.

Victoria agreed, "Oh, I think she is wonderful!"

They continued their walk.

Victoria went on. "She is very petite, and the auburn hair with the blue eyes is just delightful. Her hair is very short, but she probably has to do that because she doesn't have thirty or forty-five minutes each morning to fix it. I know she is a little … wide in the … bottom area—

"Mom, stop it please. I don't want to talk about this."

"—but that might only mean that she is going to have an easier time delivering her babies."

"Mom, just stop it."

"I'm just trying to be helpful. Wouldn't it be something if you met the love of your life on a vacation in Italy?"

Mark twisted his face into the fiercest stink-eye he could muster and threw it at his mother. "Just. Stop. It."

"That would be so romantic and a fun story to tell."

"Mom, this is real life. This is reality now. We are not in one of your Hallmark movies. This is not one of your J. Courtney Hilderbrand books."

"Yeah, sure."

They continued in silence. As they approached the restaurant, they happened upon Angelo, who had just emerged from a wine bar. They greeted him.

Angelo pointed toward the wine bar and said, "Best *Aperitivo* in Sorrento."

Victoria nodded in agreement, even though Mark knew she had no idea what an *Aperitivo* was.

"It's like a Happy Hour back in the U.S.," he told her. "Drinks and food. Though I am sure it is better than the bar food back home."

They all walked together toward the restaurant. Mark looked ahead. The *piazza* was crowded, and the outdoor seating at the restaurant was busy. He saw several people from their tour group. "Look, there's the Parks and the Collins."

As he started to point, Mark saw a boy reach across the railing and snatch a phone. A woman stood up and screamed, "My phone! Stop him!" It was Becca.

The boy started running. Becca screamed again, "He's got my phone. Stop him!"

David and Charles scrambled to their feet. Mark started running after the boy, who was a good twenty yards ahead of him. Angelo started after him at the same time.

The boy looked at Mark running at him and bumped into an old man. They both stumbled to the ground. Mark was closing fast, as was Angelo. The boy jumped up and started running again. The old man stayed on the ground, obviously shaken. Mark chased after the boy, and, looking back, saw that Angelo stopped to help the old man up.

He saw the boy's curly black hair flopping as he ran. Mark could see better now, and the boy looked to be a taller, skinny teenager. We wore tight blue jeans and a grayish shirt. Mark was a jogger and felt like he was in really good shape. So, he expected that he could run the boy down. He hadn't factored in the crowd he would have to dodge while doing so. He saw the boy turn a corner to the left, and he followed him, trying his best to avoid collisions with the tourists and townspeople. His eye caught the flopping hair again, and he saw that he was gaining ground. Then the boy turned to the right at the next block. Mark felt himself blowing and breathing hard. He was OK with a short burst, but maybe he wasn't in as good a condition as he thought. He turned the corner to the right. There was no sign of the boy. The crowd was a bit thinner, and Mark scanned the street.

Nothing. He had lost him. Becca's phone would be lost forever. He bent over and rested his hands on his knees.

Disgusted, he turned around and went back to the restaurant. Walking this time and, to his disappointment, struggling to slow down his breathing. He would have to get back on the treadmill.

After several minutes he was back at the restaurant. As he approached, he saw a crowd gathered around Angelo and the old man. The Parks and Collins were there, as well as Victoria. Looking closer, he saw that Angelo was holding the old man, but not in a supporting way. More of a restraining way. Two police officers were approaching as well.

Mark announced to them all, "Sorry, I couldn't catch him. He got away from me."

Victoria, grinning, said, "No worries. Angelo got the phone back."

"Huh?"

Angelo replied, "It was a two-person operation. The boy snatches the phone and hands it off right away to this guy. That way if the boy is caught, he claims innocence and he doesn't have the phone on him. And this one melts off into the crowd. The handoff has to be smooth, though. This one wasn't because Mrs. Park screamed, and you started after him. In the excitement he bumped into his partner," Angelo was full on laughing now, "and knocked him down. He made the handoff, but it was very clumsy. If you had caught the boy, he wouldn't have had the phone."

The two police officers arrived, and Angelo talked to them in Italian for several minutes. Angelo took out his wallet and showed it to the officers. They shook hands with Angelo and thanked him.

"So, I chased him for nothing?"

"You couldn't have known," Angelo said.

David spoke up, "Thank you both for doing this. That would have been awful to lose the phone."

"Yes, thank you," Becca said.

Mark was still trying to absorb it all. "How did you know that the two were working together?"

Angelo smiled. "I used to be a police officer. Rome. It is a common method. Pickpockets use it too."

Mark saw Becca get stiff, and she seemed to stare at Angelo. The two officers were waiting to talk with Becca, probably to take some kind of statement. But she was looking at Angelo very strangely, probably in awe. Just as Mark was. Becca also seemed to look at Charles several times. Becca's eyes were flitting. Charles, then Angelo, then Charles, then David, then Mark, then Charles, then Angelo. Poor thing is probably in shock. Really disoriented. Almost lost her phone.

Chapter 10

Pompeii

Tuesday, May 21, 2019

Mellow

Mellow walked up to the coach and noticed immediately that it had been washed. Angelo was helping the hotel porters load the suitcases. Mellow exchanged *buongiornos* with him and Angelo said, "All gassed up and ready to go."

"The coach looks really good."

"*Grazie.*"

"*Prego.*"

Their departure had to be adjusted. Late Monday, Mellow had received a text from the new local guide in Pompeii that a Norwegian cruise ship had docked in Naples and there would be thousands at the Pompeii ruins on Tuesday. She knew that this meant trouble for her group. Lines would be longer, it would be noisier, and they would probably be late for their lunch in Naples and, then, late arriving in Rome.

So, she scrambled on Monday night. She adjusted the luggage

pull from 6:45 to 6:30, kept the breakfast opening at 6:30, and moved the departure from 8:00 to 7:30.

She had called Angelo to inform him, instead of just a text. While he was still frosty with her, their relationship, such as it was, had progressed to the point of a voice call instead of a text message. Angelo had understood completely. He also told her about the incident with Becca Park and her phone. She said that she was surprised that Mark had chased the thief. Angelo had said, "I'm not. Typical American. Takes charge and they think they can do anything"

"I suppose," Mellow had said, not wanting to either agree or disagree.

"It's not a complaint. I like it. I wish Italians were more like that."

With the new times for their trip to Pompeii, Mellow hand-wrote personal notes for each of the guests, then she went through the hotel and slipped them under their doors. She also left a voice message for each, informing them of the changes.

After a quick breakfast in her own room—juice, expresso, and two of Momma Moretti's chocolate *sfogliatella*—she walked through the breakfast area to do a count of heads. She saw all of the guests except Marsha Wells and Monica Barnes, the companions from Aventura, Florida. So, she called their room. Marsha answered. They had gotten the messages and would be down shortly. "It takes Monica forever to get ready for anything! Hahahaha. We'll be down soon."

Now it looked like the early departure was under control. One final task. She changed out the seating chart that was taped to the inside front door, and she went onto the coach and moved the nametags to the new, rotated spots. Finally done. Finished as some of the guests arrived to board the coach. Whew!

Once underway, Mellow took to the PA.

"*Buongiorno!*"

She got an avalanche of boisterous *buongiornos* in reply. She smiled and complimented them on their Italian.

"Now, first off, I understand that some thanks are in order. Many of you have heard, I'm sure, about the excitement at dinner last night. For those who have not heard, let me fill you in. Last night, Becca had her phone stolen right off the table at an outdoor restaurant at *Piazza Tasso*. Fortunately, our very own Mark and Angelo were nearby. They gave chase, and, long story short, apprehended the thief and got Becca's phone back."

She heard a loud round of "Oh My's" and "Oh Lord's". Evidently, it was not widely known.

"So, let's have a round of applause for our two heroes."

The group obliged. And Becca and David clapped the loudest. Mellow made a mental note to herself to pull Mark aside in Pompeii and tell him to never do that again. It is not worth it to try to chase down a thief. You never know what you will get yourself into. It is far safer to just replace the phone. She wouldn't tell him that she had smiled to herself when she imagined Mark, dad-bod and all, trying to run down a teenager.

She would spare Angelo the lecture. He wasn't a guest. And she hadn't known that he had been with the *Polizia*.

"And thank you for your flexibility on the time change for today. I learned later last night that there is a cruise ship docked in Naples, and I am 99% certain that they will have an excursion to Pompeii. That means thousands and thousands of tourists, on top of the couple thousand that would be there anyway. I have been there when the cruise excursions invade and," she shook her head slowly from side to side, "it is not a pretty site. So, we are going to get there ahead of them."

"After Pompeii, we have a special treat for lunch. More about that later. After lunch, we will drive on to Rome. We should arrive late in the afternoon. Now, to get ready for Pompeii, I want to explain the Whispers sets we will be using."

Then she distributed the Whispers wireless audio headsets. Each consisted of a receiver, an earpiece, and a lanyard to hang over the guests' necks. She explained how to work them, one dial for volume and one dial for channel. She had already checked that all of the receivers were set to Channel 4 and so she ran a sound-check. She spoke into her Whispers microphone and a thumbs up meant that each person was able to hear her.

"For some of the stops, we will be using local guides and we will use the Whispers for those stops. They will allow you to hear the guide even if you are a hundred yards away. And the guide will not have to talk any louder than a normal conversational volume. We'll have them for Pompeii, Rome, Assisi, Florence, and Venice. Italy is very strict on the licensing of guides. They must go through thorough training and pass tests to be licensed. Only one in ten pass the exams, both written and oral. The certification programs can run twenty hours a week for a full year. Tourism is a huge part of the Italian economy and they take tourism very seriously. People who narrate tours without being licensed for that particular city can get in big, big trouble. They pay huge fines. And we don't want to get in trouble with the Italian authorities."

Chapter 11

Pompeii

Tuesday, May 21, 2019

Becca

Throughout the visit to Pompeii, David struggled to keep up with Maria, the local guide, and the rest of the group. The hand-off from Mellow to Maria was efficient and smooth, and Maria took charge of the group right away. It began with a long walk up an inclined ramp to get to the ruins. Maria warned that the ruins were just that. Ruins. And not to expect gelato stands, water fountains, restrooms, or gift shops. Like Mellow, she warned about the uneven streets.

It was clear to Becca from the start that David would struggle with the walking. The long incline tired him out, but he was determined to keep up with the group. Good. He would probably need an extra pain pill over lunch. She would be happy to oblige, after, of course, her heartfelt protestations about it. For those at their table, she would again play the concerned and worried spouse.

Becca had seen Mellow and Maria talking quietly to each other before Mellow introduced her and handed over the Whispers microphone. She figured Mellow was telling her about seeing her with Charles in Amalfi. The woman had said that she wouldn't say anything to anyone, but here she was probably gossiping about the incident. Maria did not look at Becca, but that probably just meant that Mellow told her not to look. Of course, she would tell people. Just like she probably told Angelo. Those two were talking quite a bit each time Becca and David approached the coach.

Maria came over the Whispers, "As we walk down these streets, I want you to notice two things. First is that the roads are crowned. The builders actually crowned the roads so that rain would run off and not create large puddles in the road. And also notice the deep ruts in the streets. These are from the chariots, believe it or not. The ruts are from several hundred years of chariots going up and down the streets."

Becca was only half-listening. She was preoccupied with what to do about Mellow. And she would have to do something about it before Mellow ran off at the mouth with even more people. Why oh why did she agree to duck into the alley with Charles. Couldn't he wait? Dammit.

"We are in the Forum. The Forum was the central political and economic area of Pompeii. Kind of like its downtown area. Now this building straight ahead is the Temple of Jupiter and at the time was the most magnificent structure in Pompeii."

Becca decided that she would have to deal with Mellow. And quickly. David seemed to be sinking fast. His breathing while he was sleeping was very labored and deep. He could go any day now. Even quicker if he insisted on more pain pills. And certainly once she slipped him the Clonazepam. Yes, she could not have Mellow around. But what to do?

"And behind the Temple of Jupiter are the public baths. These, as you'll see, were quite ornate. There were separate areas for men and women, of course. And the baths had both hot and cold water. I will give you some time to explore these. Let's meet right back here in ten minutes. Then, we'll walk to some of the private residences."

Becca saw that Victoria and Mark, as well as the two women from Florida were within earshot.

"Honey, why don't we just sit here and rest for a while?" she said to David. "There's a bench right here."

"No, I want to go in and see this. It's pretty interesting. Seems so modern."

"I think the rest will do you good."

"I'll rest later. We have the ride to Rome, you know."

Becca glanced over at Victoria, and gave her a frown and a subtle shrug of her shoulders, as if saying "what am I going to do?"

Victoria nodded her sympathy. Satisfied, Becca led David into the ruins of the baths.

After the public baths, Maria led them for several blocks to the House of Vettii. On the way, she again brought up the chariot ruts.

"Here is an interesting factoid about these ruts you see. Many of you may not know that the first roads built in England were by the Romans. And those were designed, like all roads throughout the Roman Empire, for chariots. When the British built their first railroads, they used a railroad gauge that matches up exactly to the distance between the wheels of a chariot. Scientists from England have been here to measure the distance between the ruts, and they found that it matches almost exactly to the four feet, eight inches of the standard British railroads."

David asked, "How did the chariots end up at four feet, eight inches?"

Becca was surprised at the question. David had struggled to keep up with the walking. But he was listening.

"Great question. Legend has it that it goes back to Julius Caesar. He set the width to be the distance of two strides of one of his soldiers. Then again, there are people who say that the whole chariot-rut-railroad story is a bunch of hooey."

They arrived at the House of Vettii, and Maria went on to explain the significance of the residence. The House of Vettii was one of the best-preserved houses in Pompeii. It was owned by two merchants who used it to show off their wealth.

Becca was barely listening, but she saw that David was rallying. He was listening intently, and he seemed to have more energy. Her mood soured. She was frustrated: why did everything had to be so hard?

Maria gave the group time to explore the House on their own, making a point to call out all of the fresco painting on the walls. "It is amazing that these have survived for 2000 years."

Becca and David explored the House, and Becca was surprised that she herself found it so interesting. As an interior decorator, she was impressed with the care and thought that was put into the house.

Maria then ended her narrated tour. She told them that Mellow would meet them, in thirty minutes, at the *Porta Marina*, the entrance that they had used upon their arrival. If they have time, she said, they should look over the plaster casts housed near the gate.

While walking back to the entrance, Becca saw that the Kastner group was swarmed over with another group of about 70 or 80 Asian tourists. Maybe a hundred. They were traveling as a group, behind a guide who carried a large blue flag on a pole. He was walking quickly, and the group was hustling to keep up. He stopped a couple of times, for no longer than 30 seconds each time, and practically screamed his explanation to the group. The group had no Whispers devices or their equivalents. Becca did not recognize the language but figured maybe a third of them could actually hear him, despite his shouting.

Maria was walking beside Becca and David. She smiled at them and said, "That's the excursion from the cruise ship in Naples. And that's just the first. I'm sure there will be another three or four groups just like them within the next hour."

David replied, "You were very smart to move our time up. Nicely done."

"And I will bet that he is not a licensed guide."

Mellow was waiting as they arrived at the gate. Early, as usual.

Chapter 12

Rome

Tuesday, May 21, 2019

Mellow

Mellow ushered the last guest onto the coach, and she turned to board herself.

Angelo stopped her. "Are you sure you want to go to Naples? It is not the kind of place that Kastner usually goes to."

"What do you mean by that?" Mellow knew *exactly* what he meant. She just wanted him to have to explain himself, to see if he would be embarrassed by his bias.

"Well, Melanie and I would normally just stop for lunch further on the way to Rome. We never went into Naples. It's not a stop on any of the Kastner tours. Or anyone else's for that matter."

"I added it to the itinerary. It's a quick stop for lunch. In and out. And at an historic restaurant."

"Does Zurich know you added it?"

Mellow looked into Angelo's challenging eyes and weighed her reply. She had not told Luca about the addition. She wanted to say,

Why don't you just get off of my back and just drive? I am in charge of the itinerary. Not you. But that would obviously just escalate the conflict. An escalation she couldn't afford.

"I don't understand your concern about Naples." She did her best to show innocence in her tone and facial expression.

Angelo let out a deep sigh. "Alright, you're going to make me say it, so I will. It's a dirty town, it's congested, and it has lots and lots of crime. The Mafia still runs it. And, in case you haven't kept up on the news, it is full of toxic waste dumps, including nuclear waste. Why would you take tourists there?"

Mellow was surprised. She thought he would back down since it was socially inappropriate to talk about Naples like that. To say it out loud. Even though it was how a lot of Italians felt.

She stared blankly at him. He stared back, waiting for her reply.

"So, are you refusing to drive us there?" Mellow hadn't answered his question about whether or not she had the approval of the Kastner office in Zurich. So, Angelo couldn't be sure that she hadn't. Plus, the over-riding rule at Kastner Tours is that the Tour Director is in charge of the Tour; the driver's role is to just drive safely and efficiently.

She waited only two seconds for his reply, and then she started up the steps. He gave a meek, "Of course not," and followed her.

On board, she was pleased with the buzz of conversation among the guests. She took to the PA.

"We have a special treat for lunch today. Before we head to Rome, we are going to take a quick trip into Naples for a lunch you would probably never ever get on another tour." She paused for effect. "But, before I explain the lunch, let me tell you about Naples. Many tour groups bypass Naples. To many, it is considered the least desirable of the Italian cities. It is seen by many as being crowded and dirty, with a lot of crime." She dropped a glance over to Angelo, who kept his eyes forward.

"I don't think that is the case. I think Naples is one of the hidden gems of Italy. It is crowded and noisy with a lot of narrow roads with laundry flapping on the line. I would call it *gritty*. With a lot of atmosphere and character." She heard a few chuckles, and she went on. "As far as crime goes, it has more crime than other cities in Europe, but it is almost all petty crime. Naples has far less crime than, say, Chicago or Baltimore. And a lot less violent crime than the typical American big city."

She again paused to look the group over. They were all alert and attentive, some sneaking glances out the window as Angelo was now on the E45 Toll road to Naples.

"Now, about lunch. Naples is known as having the best pizza in the world. And we are going to eat at the restaurant that is recognized as the place that *invented* pizza. *The Pizzeria Brandi*. Here's a pop quiz. How did the margherita pizza get its name?"

Victoria shot her hand up, "Oh, Oh, I know. I know."

Mellow called on her.

"It's named after the drink. The Margarita!"

Many in the group giggled, but Victoria went on, "It must have tequila in the dough."

"Sorry, Victoria, that's not correct. It is named after Queen Margherita. Here is the story. By the late 1800s, pizza was already becoming popular in Naples and others in Italy were curious about it. Queen Margherita visited Naples and expressed interest in trying the new food. Her entourage went to the *Pizzeria Brandi*. The chef made up a new one, just for her. Legend has it that he chose to represent the three colors of the new flag of Italy. Tomatoes for red, mozzarella for white, and basil for green. Hence the Margherita Pizza."

Arjun, from Columbia, Maryland, shouted out, "You are making this up." The entire coach laughed.

"I swear to god that I am not. It is a true story. You will see for yourself when we get to the restaurant. If you are not a pizza lover, don't worry. They have a full menu."

Arjun turned to his wife, "She has to be making this up."

Mellow noticed that Angelo had turned off of the road too early;

they were heading toward the Federico University. She looked over at him. His eyes were focused forward. She saw that Angelo had not turned on the onboard navigation system. She figured that he was unaware that he had made a wrong turn. She thought about saying something to him but decided to bite her tongue. It was so hard.

She decided to go along with it. She announced to the group, "We are heading toward the Federico University." She thought that her statement might alert Angelo that he was on the wrong route.

"The Federico University has 80,000 students and is one of the largest in Italy. It was founded way back in the year 1200 by Federico the Second, who was one of the Holy Roman Emperors."

Angelo stopped at an intersection, and Mellow saw him looking around. She knew he needed to turn right to get back on route to the Pizzeria Brandi. She pursed her lips and held her tongue.

After several moments, Angelo turned again and Mellow let out a controlled sigh. They were on the correct street, the *Via Toledo*. The restaurant was about a mile ahead.

"Federico was known for his support of literature, the arts, and science. I will be quiet for a while and let you appreciate the architecture of the buildings, a great mix of old and new."

A minute later, Angelo turned right and proceeded into the Spanish Quarter. He should have kept straight; the restaurant had been only a mile ahead. Mellow wondered if he did it on purpose. She looked over at him. No, he hadn't. His head was swiveling, as if looking for some kind of landmark. Or street sign. As it was, they were heading into the thick of one of the least desirable neighborhoods in Naples. Known for drug dealers, crime, and prostitution.

In any other situation, she would have walked up to the driver, pointed out the wrong turn, and given exact instructions on how to get back to the correct route. Even if it meant a minor embarrassment to the driver. Having to be the New Mellow, she couldn't.

She also noticed several guests looking out the window and

murmuring to their seatmates. She had to do something. She took the microphone in hand and turned on the PA.

"Angelo has taken a slight detour into what's known as the Spanish Quarter. It is named that because it was where the Spanish troops were stationed back in the 1600s when Spain ruled this area. I told you that Naples was gritty. Well, the Spanish Quarter exemplifies that. Some of these streets and alleys are only 10 feet wide."

She glanced over at Angelo. He was again looking side to side, concern on his face.

"If you are getting hungry, don't worry. Angelo is only two right turns from being back on the road to the *Pizzeria Brandi*. It was only about a mile from where we turned off the *Via Toledo*."

Angelo took the next right turn, without looking back at Mellow.

"You are getting to see an authentic part of Italy that few tourists ever get to see."

Angelo took another right and they were once again on the *Via Toledo*.

Mellow let out another slow, suppressed sigh.

Within minutes they pulled up to disembark the coach. They were only about 15 minutes later than they should have been.

Once inside, they were directed to a separate eating area. There were multiple tables for six and eight. Mellow settled into a table with James and Kecia. Moments later, Arjun and Maya joined them.

Arjun said, "Mellow, I stand corrected. I saw all of the plaques and signs in the lobby. Your story about Queen Margherita is true. My apologies. I won't doubt you on anything else for the rest of the trip."

Victoria and Mark were at the next table, and Victoria let out a loud laugh when she ordered. Mellow looked over at her, as did many at the nearby tables.

Victoria, noticing that many were now looking at her, proclaimed, loudly, "I ordered a margarita with my Margherita Pizza."

Mark dropped his chin and shook his head.

Mellow was pleased with the lunch. The restaurant proved to be a great success. Most had the Margherita Pizza, which the consensus declared as melt-in-the-mouth good. Some of the men had the more-filling sausage and pepperoni pizzas and washed them down with Nastro Azzurro beer.

Victoria liked the pizza, but not the drink. The bartender used limoncello instead of an orange liqueur, which made the drink rather sour. "It's unique," Victoria had said. Then she didn't finish it.

They left Pizzeria Brandi at about 1:30, and Mellow figured that they would be in Rome in a couple of hours, provided Angelo followed the best route. She thought about telling him, or asking maybe, to turn on the onboard navigation. But she didn't.

Once underway on the A1 expressway, Mellow took to the PA system to give her initial talk on Rome. She said that they would be making a rest stop about halfway there. Summer Rooms would be available.

She explained that they had a three-page summary in their packet, but that she would give the highlights. She covered the founding with the legend of Romulus and Remus, the role of the Etruscans and the Greeks, and the rise of the Roman Empire.

Then, she covered the most significant Roman Emperors. Julius Caesar, Augustus, Nero, Hadrian, Marcus Aurelius, and Constantine.

"Marcus Aurelius was my favorite and, I believe, the most underrated. Have any of you read his *Meditations*?"

She looked down the coach. Only Mark had his hand up, and only slightly at that.

"His *Meditations* were a private journal he kept while campaigning and conquering parts of eastern Europe. They formed the foundation for what is known as the Stoic school of philosophy. I have another handout of the best quotes from his *Meditations*."

She walked down the aisle and distributed the handout to each of them.

Going back on the PA, she said, "Stoicism is very misunderstood. Stoic philosophy is not about being unemotional. It is more about accepting things and being very mindful about how you react to events in your life. Existentialism of the twentieth century and modern day cognitive behavioral theory have a lot of their roots in the ancient Stoic philosophers."

She scanned the group and saw that only about a third of them were listening closely, especially Mark, and James and Kecia Jackson. She was surprised, pleasantly, that Mark, unlike earlier drives, did not have his nose in his phone. Usually after lunch, a lot of the guests would be nodding off in their seats. She figured that she was doing good to have the attention of a third of them. So, she pressed on.

"Let me read you the two quotes that I like the best. The first is *Do not indulge in dreams of having what you have not but reckon up the chief of the blessings you do possess, and then thankfully remember how you would crave for them if they were not yours.* My father would always tell me that the biggest problem people have is that they always want more than they currently have. He used to say, 'why can't people want what they have instead of wanting what they don't have?' This quote is, I think, at the heart of Stoicism."

She saw that the same guests were still attentive.

"And this second one is my favorite of all time. *Look well into thyself; there is a source of strength which will always spring up if thou wilt always look.* I think what he is saying is that you are stronger than you think you are and that, with persistence, you can get through almost any of life's challenges."

Not wanting to overdo it, and not wanting to look like she was doing personal recruiting to her Stoicism, Mellow decided it would be best to move on.

"OK, let me tell you about the next few days. Today is a long day, and we started early. So, we are taking it easy for the first night in Rome. We should arrive late afternoon. We are staying at the *Viaggiatore Rilassante*, which, translated, means the *Relaxing Traveler*. It is known locally as the *Rilassante*, so we will call it that. It is in a very nice area, only a few blocks from the Spanish Steps and the high-end shopping of the *Via Condotti*. The *Via Condotti* is in the same category as Fifth Avenue in New York, North Michigan Avenue in Chicago, and Rodeo Drive in LA.

"Dinner is on your own at the *Ristorante Galetti*. It is just down the street from the *Rilassante*. You can order anything you want from the menu. But alcoholic drinks are on your dollar. Or Euro. Then, we will do a nighttime visit to Trevi Fountain and then drive past the Vatican to see it lit up. These are both amazing at night when they are all lit up."

"We will plan to meet at 8:30 in the lobby to drive there. Before that, I should tell you that the Spanish Steps give you wonderful views of Rome. I plan to be there myself at sunset. It's spectacular to see Rome from the top of the steps. Especially as the sun is setting."

"In the morning we will have a coach tour of the historic parts of Rome. Then, we will go to the Vatican for a tour. I will tell you more tonight when we go on the evening tour."

By 4:00 they were in the outskirts of Rome. Mellow did not recognize the route that Angelo was taking, and it seemed to her to be out of the way. She decided that she had to say something. Lost in Naples was one thing. But, lost in Rome could put them hours behind schedule. It was time for the Old Mellow. She approached Angelo, "I am not familiar with this route. I am not sure that this is the best way to the *Rilassante*."

Angelo broke into a broad grin, "No, you have to trust me on this one, Mellow. I was with the *Polizia* for nine years in Rome. I know it very well." They were stopped at a light, and he turned his head to her and said, very softly, "I know I got lost in Naples. I'd never been to that restaurant before. Melanie never took a group there. But I do know Rome."

The light turned and they started off again.

"You are absolutely certain? You don't want to turn on the navigation system?"

"Don't need it." Angelo then rattled off the street names he would be taking, along with which ones were left turns and which were right turns. Mellow couldn't follow him. She looked around and had no idea where they were.

"Alright, just checking."

"By the way," again a near whisper, "thank you for not pointing out that I got lost. If you see me doing that again, please get me back to the correct route."

"You got it." Mellow noticed that Angelo had called her "Mellow" for the first time. She sat back and watched as Angelo navigated the side streets of Rome.

After fifteen minutes, he made a right turn and Mellow suddenly recognized that they were near the Villa Borghese, less than a mile from the *Rilassante*. Amazing.

They pulled into the *Rilassante* at 4:15, a half-hour earlier than Mellow had expected.

She gave Angelo a whispered, "Nicely done."

They were quickly off the coach and settled into their rooms. Mellow had a room on the third floor. It was a quick walk up from the lobby. She wouldn't be slowed by waiting for elevators.

She had called the Hotel Manager, Aldo Capuzzi, and told him to give the guests the better rooms on the higher floors. Those had window views, and, even better, stairway access to a rooftop that provided spectacular views of the city.

The first thing she noticed when she entered her room was the statue of Marcus Aurelius. It sat prominently on the coffee table. Mellow went over and picked it up. Heavy. She needed both hands to lift it. It looked just like the one they used to have in the lobby. Next to it was a bottle of Brunello, with an opener and wine glass.

She went to her phone and called the Front Desk. *"Buona Sera.* This is Mellow in Room 302. Is Aldo available?"

He came on moments later. *"Buona sera,* Mellow."

"Aldo, I just checked in and noticed the statue of Marcus Aurelius. Did you do that?"

"Indeed, Mellow, I have. I know how much you think of him, so I had him moved to your room for the length of your stay."

"It's the one that you had in the lobby? I noticed it was missing."

"Yes, indeed it is."

"Well, that is very thoughtful of you. It is much appreciated. As is the Brunello."

Mellow's thoughts jumped back to the time she shared a bottle of Brunello with Aldo in the Hotel bar. Probably 5 years ago. It was then they learned they shared Stoicism as a philosophy of life, and of their taste for Brunello. It was good to find a fellow Stoic. They had shared their favorite quotes from Seneca, Epictetus, and, of course, Marcus Aurelius.

Aldo was a long-time friend of her father. They knew each other from the Embassy days. Her father in the U.S. Embassy in Berlin. Aldo in the Italian Embassy. The two had gotten very close over the years. To the point where Mellow called him *Uncle Aldo* while she was growing up. He had retired a few years before her father, and he settled into managing the *Rilassante*. Mellow hadn't talked with him since he came to her father's funeral back in February.

Mellow checked her watch. She had time to shower, eat dinner, and do some prep work for the next day. And she had calls to make to check up on the Assisi plans.

But she had one more question for Aldo. "Are you sure you don't have any more information about my father?"

There was a long pause, very long for Aldo's style.

"I'm sorry, Mellow. I wish there was more that I could tell you. But there isn't."

"OK. Just thought I would ask." She still thought that Aldo was holding back.

"Now you know that if you need absolutely anything while you are in Rome you just have to call me. Right?"

"Yes, I do. Thanks."

She took a scarf from her spinner and walked over to the statue. Tying the scarf loosely around its neck, she asked, "Well, Mr. Aurelius. What do you think? Stylish?"

Just before 8:00, Mellow left for the Spanish Steps. The air was clear and cool. She was not exaggerating when she had told the guests that it was her favorite view of the city. Her ritual was to walk to the top and look back to the west to watch the sun set. And, since it was May, the Steps would be adorned with pink azaleas. You could look down at the rooftops of the four and five story buildings, with St. Peters on the far horizon. It was not to be missed. She would have added it to the itinerary, but many of the Kastner guests would have a difficult time climbing the 135 steps. Like Amalfi, no railings, uneven steps, and very dangerous for unsteady climbers. It was the equivalent of walking up the steps of a ten-story building.

She walked along the *Via Condotti*. She couldn't afford any of the merchandise, but she gazed at the windows of Michael Kors, Tiffany, and Ferragamo. She continued on past Bulgari, Jimmy Choo, and Louis Vuitton. Ridiculous.

The street ended at the Spanish Steps. The crowd thickened as she approached. She figured there were at least a couple thousand people at the Steps and *Piazza*. It was popular with both tourists and locals. She could see the rows of azaleas as she approached. They seemed to be on every step on both sides of the Steps, forming solid pink lines that broke the Steps into thirds.

Getting closer, she found herself just in front of the *Fontana della Barcaccia*, the "Fountain of the Boat". A throng of people surrounded the fountain, with some going up and actually drinking from the spouts. The water was said to be safe, but Mellow had never tried it. Too disgusting. She heard a street musician strumming his guitar. Farther away, a saxophone. To the right sat a white and black *Polizia* car. It seemed like a permanent fixture, as it was in the same place each time she visited. She thought that maybe they just parked it there to fake people out. As she looked up at the hoard of people sitting on the Steps, she remembered hearing that the authorities were considering banning people from sitting on the them. Too crowded, they said, with people struggling to walk the Steps and having to dodge the squatters. Yeah, good luck with that. She looked up and she saw clusters of people sitting with their gelatos. It was so packed she couldn't see a straight path up. As usual.

She started up the Steps near the middle. To make progress she had to step between groups, then to the right, then a few steps to the left, then up a couple of steps, then to the right again. And so it went. She could smell the azaleas as she progressed.

Halfway up, the Steps took a major turn to the right, or the left, then went up again to the first of two lookout areas. She stopped momentarily at the lower lookout. Still not high enough. She wanted the higher lookout, where she could see the tops of the buildings.

Finally at the top, with a few hundred of her fellow gawkers, she looked out over Rome. The sun was just above the horizon. To the right she could see the red and white flag at the headquarters of the Order of Malta, with the oversized Church *Sant'Ambrogio e San Carlo al Corso* just behind it. Farther on the horizon stood the dome of St. Peter's Basilica. With the sun just now setting, it was stunning. She stood there for several minutes just to take it all in. She noticed that the buzz of conversation in the crowd had died down. The entire crowd sat in reverent quiet and took in the sunset.

Once the sun went down, she checked her watch. She had about twenty minutes to get back and get ready for the evening trip to Trevi and St. Peter's Square. So, she started down the Steps. Now it seemed even more crowded than before and, going down, she had to be especially mindful of where she was stepping.

She progressed down past the lower lookout and was at the top of the lower section. The only possible path down seemed to be in the middle. So, she stepped to her left and started to walk down the middle.

She took three steps down and had her right leg in mid-air when she felt a push from behind. She plunged several steps down, narrowly avoiding several gelato-lovers on her right. On pure reflex, she put her hands out, but her left arm caught on the back of someone sitting. The left side of her forehead smashed into a lower step, and her knee hit solid stone. She heard several people shouting just before she passed out.

Chapter 13

Rome

Tuesday, May 21, 2019

Mark

Mark and Victoria spent some time reviewing Mellow's list of recommended restaurants. Mark went online and pulled up a few menus. After both had weighed in, they settled on the *Ristorante Galetti*, the restaurant that was already included in their tour. The *Galetti* was only a few blocks from the hotel, just on the other side of the *Via Condotti*. It only took a few minutes to walk there, even with the throngs of people on the street.

As they entered, Mark saw James and Kecia Jackson arrive from the opposite direction.

Mark greeted them, "Hello, strangers," and he held the door for them. James insisted on allowing Victoria to go first.

Once inside, Victoria asked, "Do you two want to join us for dinner?"

James and Kecia looked at each other very briefly, then both said, "Of course."

Mark motioned them to walk in ahead of them, and he hung back momentarily to sneak a peek at his phone. Still did not get the email or text he was expecting. Aggravating. He took a breath and told himself to be more patient.

While they were reviewing their menus, David asked, "So how are you enjoying the trip so far?"

"This has been fantastic," Kecia said. "It's even better than we would have imagined."

They compared their impressions. The views in Sorrento were amazing. As was the drive on the Amalfi Coast. The food has been wonderful. Rome is *so* congested. But there is lots to see.

Kecia proclaimed, "I think I could live in Italy."

The server came and they placed their orders. Victoria ordered lasagna, Kecia had the tagliolini with ham, and both James and David asked for the salmon with pesto risotto. Mark ordered a bottle of wine, a Barolo, once he learned that James and Kecia preferred reds. Otherwise, he would have had to order a lesser wine by the glass.

While they ate, Victoria said to Kecia, "I have to tell you, I just really love the scarves. I think Mellow is right, you always feel dressed up when you wear one."

"I think she said that Florence was a great place to buy them," Kecia said.

"But I don't think I can wait that long," Victoria said.

Kecia went on, "We have been on several tours with Kastner, and the tour director makes all of the difference. We are really liking Mellow. What do you think of her so far?"

Mark saw that Victoria snuck him a quick glance before saying, "I think she is delightful."

James added, "Yes, she is really good. A bit high strung. She is always moving, always checking on things. But she is very organized and obviously very knowledgeable. I would have to give her an A so far."

"That seems to be the consensus," Mark said. "And I would agree."

Later, as they left the restaurant, James and Kecia decided that they would check out some of the shops on the *Via Condotti*. Victoria and Mark started back to the hotel.

Along the way, Mark spotted a small wine shop. Somehow he had missed it on their earlier walk to the restaurant. Against Victoria's objections, he insisted that they stop in. "Just to see what they have."

They ended up staying for half an hour. Inside, Mark saw separate sections for a wide variety of Italian wines. Piedmont, Tuscany, Veneto, Campagna, Sicily. He took out his phone and began to snap photos of labels. The shop also had sections for French and German wines. Even a section for Napa Cabs.

In an *Other* section, he even found a few bottles of cabernet sauvignon from Horse Heaven Hills in Washington State. He figured that must be for the un-adventuresome American tourists.

He went back to Victoria, who had found a chair to rest on. Getting her attention, he said, "I am in heaven."

He could see that she was completely bored. So, he wrapped up the visit by buying a few bottles of Barolo – the same brand that he had just enjoyed at *Ristorante Galetti*. He had no idea when he would drink them, but he felt obliged to buy them. The proprietor had been so helpful and accommodating.

As they stood to leave, Victoria caught the attention of the cashier and asked, "Excuse me. Could I use your Summer Room?"

The cashier wrinkled his brow, "*Scusi*. Excuse me."

"You know, your ... Summer Rooms. I really have to go. I don't think I can make it back to our hotel."

The cashier turned to Mark with complete confusion on his face. Mark smiled at him. "She means *bagno*."

"Oh, of course. Allow me to show you where it is."

On the way to the back of the shop, Mark explained to Victoria that *Summer Rooms* was just a euphemism that Mellow was using for the tour. It is not a real expression used in Italy.

Victoria put her head back and let out one of her boisterous hyena laughs.

She said, "Well, I bet that clerk must think I am some kind of crazy American tourist."

"I'll bet you are right."

They returned to the *Rilassante* and made their way to the lobby. Mellow had set 8:30 as the departure time and they were early. Victoria spotted the piano in the lobby and walked over to it. She opened the bench and found several pieces of sheet music. Mark saw her shaking her head. She put the music back and sat down, clearly not finding anything to her liking.

She looked over at Mark, who gave her a nod and said, "Go ahead."

So, she sat down and began to play. First was the theme song from "Beauty and the Beast."

The guests began to arrive, and they settled around Victoria at the piano. The music filled the lobby.

Char and Susan went over to Mark. "Wow, she is really good. No music, just playing."

Others came over, many who were not with the tour. Mark wandered to the back of the crowd. Victoria finished "Beauty and the Beast," and then nodded graciously to the clapping she had earned. Mark recognized that Victoria, as usual, gave the ending a little signature of her own.

She turned back to the piano, gave a quizzical look, and then a smile.

She started Yiruma's "River Flows in You." Again, without any sheet music.

Char asked Mark, "She knows these by heart?"

"She has been giving private lessons for twenty years. These are pieces that her students play at their recitals. Yiruma is especially popular now."

"It is so soothing," Susan said.

Next up, Victoria began Billy Joel's "Just the Way You Are," and brought more energy to the room. The crowd was larger now, maybe 25 people.

James and Kecia joined Mark. James said, "No Mellow yet. That's odd. She is always early."

"It is not like her, is it?" Mark replied.

Chapter 14

Rome

Tuesday, May 21, 2019

Mellow

Mellow felt a tug at her eyelid and then a bright light in her left eye. She blinked. The light went to her right eye, which was also then pulled open.

She heard, "*Signorina, come ti chiami?*"

She tried to talk, but it only came out as a mumble. She blinked again. Then several more times.

"Where am I?" The words came out in a slur.

"*Signorina*, what is your name?"

"Melody." Now she could understand her own speech.

She tried to sit up, but a stabbing pain in her forehead forced her back down.

"Please just lie still. You are safe. We will take care of you."

"Oh, my head."

She forced her eyes open and looked around. A man was looking into her eyes. Another was cleaning her forehead. He wiped it with something that stung her skin. Then he applied some kind of bandage.

"Where am I?"

"You are on the Spanish Steps. You had quite a fall."

"Oh, yeah." Memories started to return. Rome. Spanish Steps. Sunset. Azaleas. Have to get to the hotel.

"Try to keep this ice on your head." The ice man moved Mellow's hand to hold the ice in place.

"Is there someone we can call?"

"What happened?"

"You fell down the steps. You hit your head very hard. And your knee is scraped. It looks like you passed out for a few minutes."

"What time is it?"

"It's just after 8:30."

Mellow felt a panic come on. "I need to get to the hotel. I have a group."

"Signorina, you need to just sit and rest a moment. We need to get some ice on your knee also."

Again, the light man asked, "Is there anyone we can call?"

"Yes. Angelo. I need my phone."

The ice man moved her purse closer, and Mellow opened it. As she did, she heard her phone buzz. She looked at the caller ID. Angelo. He was calling her.

"Angelo. I'm going to be late."

"Where are you?"

"At the Spanish Steps."

"You don't sound right. Are you alright?"

"I'm not sure."

The light man put his hand on her phone, "May I?"

She gave him her phone. The man talked with Angelo, very fast and in Italian. While she listened, more of her memory started to come back. The Steps. Saw the sunset. Started back to the hotel. These are some police or medical people attending to me. I'm late for the drive to Trevi and the Vatican. Oh, my head.

The light man gave her phone back and she brought it to her ear. "Angelo?"

"He said that you hit your head and appear to have a mild concussion. Your knee is bleeding, but not bad. You need ice on your head and your knee. The people around you called for medical services to come to check you out. He is saying that you should go to the hospital for observation."

"No, I don't want to do that. I don't remember falling."

"Some of the people said that it looked like someone bumped into you from behind, or maybe even pushed you."

"Why would someone do that? Well, I don't know. I have to get back for the Trevi and Vatican drive."

"I can come and get you. Maybe we should just cancel the drive. I am sure the guests will understand."

"What are they doing now? Are they all in the lobby?"

"Yes, Victoria is playing the piano in the lobby. They are having a good time."

"The piano. In the lobby." She tried to visualize it but struggled. "I hate to cancel. That's not right."

"Well, the doctor, or whoever I talked to, said that you need to rest, and someone needs to be with you. To keep an eye on you for a while. Otherwise, I could just take the guests myself. There's no real storytelling tonight."

Mellow took several moments to collect her thoughts. She could feel the coldness of the ice on her head. And her knee. What could she do?

"Angelo, call Aldo. Ask him to come and get me." She assumed Angelo knew Aldo. Everyone at Kastner did. "Then go ahead and take them on the drive."

"I will call Aldo right away. What should I tell the guests?"

"Tell them the truth. I had a bad fall at the Spanish Steps and won't be able to make tonight's drive. I will be fine by morning."

"If you think we should." Mellow heard hesitancy in his voice. "Let me talk to the doctor again."

Mellow handed the phone over to the light man. "He wants to talk with you again."

The man took the phone and gave a professional, "*Pronto.*"

Mellow listened and could make out Angelo's voice, but not the words. It was machine-gun Italian. The light man said nothing. Then he ended the call and handed the phone back to Mellow.

"Who is Aldo?" the man asked.

"The manager at the *Rilassante*. A friend. What did Angelo say to you?"

The light man broke into a broad grin. "He said that he was with the *Polizia* and that if I let anything happen to you before Aldo gets here, he would hunt me down and give me a beating. One that I would not like."

They exchanged smiles.

"Is Angelo your boyfriend."

"No, my driver."

The light man stared at her for several seconds. "Let me check your eyes one more time." He shined his light into each. "You seem to be doing better. I still recommend that you go to the hospital. Just as a precaution."

"No hospital. I have too much to do."

"It is important that you get some rest and very important that someone stay with you. If you get nauseous, dizzy, or drowsy, you need to get medical attention right away. It might indicate that you have bleeding in your brain. You need to take this seriously."

Mellow gave him a perfunctory nod of agreement. "What can I take for this headache?"

"Tylenol. Avoid ibuprofen or aspirin. Those may increase the risk of bleeding. Whatever you do, make sure that you don't put yourself in a situation of any kind where you might get another blow to the head. Your head needs time to recover. And don't do anything strenuous."

"I understand. *Grazie.*"

Aldo arrived a few minutes later. Mellow thanked both the light man and the ice man, and Aldo brought her back to the hotel. It was a slow walk back to the *Rilassante*. Mellow's tender knee made her limp a bit, and she had to take small steps to avoid shooting pains in her head.

Once at the *Rilassante*, Aldo brought the front desk worker, Gina, along with him when he brought Mellow to her room. Gina was Aldo's daughter and scheduled for the night shift at the front desk.

Aldo said, "I will work the desk. Gina will stay with you."

Gina and Mellow knew each other from prior tours, as well as time together in Berlin when their fathers worked in their respective embassies. Gina said that she would be happy to help in any way she could. Gina was only a few years younger than Mellow.

Aldo left, saying that he would check in again in the morning.

Mellow took two Tylenol tablets, showered, and looked at her emails and text messages. Nothing that couldn't wait. She thought about calling Luca but decided she would wait until morning. It suddenly dawned on her that he might pull her from the tour. Medical reasons. But he did not have a backup. She was already the backup. Would he combine with another tour? No, there wasn't any. Except a southbound one that would cross her tour in Assisi. That wouldn't work. Maybe there is someone else that they could call in an emergency. She really didn't know. She would tell Luca not to worry, that she could continue. Luca would talk with Angelo and get his opinion. Angelo had suddenly gotten very protective. He would tell Luca that she shouldn't continue, and Luca would then scramble to find someone else to finish it. No, she would have to convince Angelo that she was alright and could continue the tour. Oh, it was all so confusing, and she couldn't think straight. She would figure it out in the morning.

She texted Angelo: *How is it going?*

He wrote back: *Leaving Vatican now. Went fine. How are you doing?*

Better. See you in the morning. Caio.

Then her mind flashed to—why would someone push me? She had no answers. It must have been an accidental bump. But she now remembered a full hand on her back just before the fall. No, it wasn't a bump, it was a push. It all made no sense. She would think about that in the morning too.

She set her phone for a 7:00 wake up alarm and went to sleep.

Chapter 15

Rome

Tuesday, May 21, 2019

Becca

Becca settled into bed next to David, satisfied with how things were going. David was sound asleep and, judging from his wheezing, he was having a hard time getting deep breaths. The second dose of the pain pill was having an effect. He had no energy after dinner and had just wanted to go back to the room and go to sleep.

She smiled, happy with the situation. Mellow fell hard after the push, much harder than Becca had expected. It was a stroke of genius to push her when she had one foot in the air, and not anchored to the stone steps. She had hit her head pretty hard, and it looked like her knee had smashed against a step.

Becca, of course, ran off in the other direction once Mellow fell. But she felt like the pushing worked. Mellow would be hurt and unable to continue on the tour. Then, Kastner would get someone else to fill in and she wouldn't have to worry about Mellow anymore. When David died of Becca's cocktail of oxycodone and Clonazepam,

Mellow would not be around for any kind of questioning. Becca would be home free.

Charles would be surprised. But then he would be free to divorce Sharon.

She was very satisfied with the progress of events. It was going to happen. Mellow would be gone. Nothing would stand in her way. She would make it happen tomorrow.

PART TWO

Chapter 16

Barrington, Illinois

Monday, October 2, 2018

Becca

Becca was not optimistic when she entered David's office. She had already talked with him about adding vintage architectural pieces to the stores. David had thoroughly rejected it. Now she was back to propose it again. Sure, she had Charles with her, but she was convinced David would say no again.

After David's initial dismissal of the idea, Becca followed up with Charles and explained what she had in mind. She vented her frustrations at how "bull-headed" David could be. She had sneered while she mimicked his objections, "It's just antiques. There's no margin. We're not an antique store. People don't want to buy someone else's old junk."

For this second attempt, Charles had helped with the proposal. And he had prepared a real business case. Charles had said, "David is a hard-headed businessman. He needs facts, figures, sales projections, margins, risk analyses." So, they set about the building of a business case. Becca marveled at how quickly Charles had pulled it together. Market analysis, cost analyses (only variable costs, since the stores themselves were already a fixed cost). And he toned it down to a pilot only, and in an existing store. Becca had proposed building two new stores focused exclusively on the new approach. And her pitch was, in retrospect, a sorry comparison to what Charles had assembled.

Charles was on her side. "At least worth a pilot tryout," he had said.

Now she was proposing it again, albeit a scaled down version. She followed Charles in, and they sat in front of David's desk. He sat there with his arms folded across his chest, but an empty expression on his face. She couldn't read it.

Then it dawned on her. He forgot about the meeting and the reason for it. His memory was getting worse. Last week, he had forgotten about a dinner party they were supposed to attend. Recently, he had complained that vendors were showing up "unexpectedly". He had forgotten their appointments. Now he just sat there, waiting for one of them, her or Charles, to say something.

Charles seemed to read the silence and began. "I called this meeting to go over a proposal we have worked on for a pilot program on selling old architectural pieces."

David came to life, "Yes, that's what we need to talk about." He twisted his chair to the credenza behind his desk and retrieved a copy of the proposal. Becca noticed that it was well-worn; wrinkled pages, dog-eared corners, and inky fingerprints. Becca and Charles each had a copy of the proposal.

David held it up and said, "I don't think we have to go through this. I really like the idea of a small pilot in one or two stores. That keeps our costs under control, and lets us see how it works. It will be easier to make whatever tweaks or adjustments we need to."

He turned to Becca, "Honey, this is so much better than what you first came up with. I mean the idea of spending a couple million dollars to build and stock new stores was just impractical." He shifted his eyes to Charles, "This almost reminds me of our plans for giving freelance interior designers desks and office space in our stores."

Becca was dumbfounded. David had agreed without even hearing their pitch. She bristled at how he called her "honey", but she said nothing. She felt her lips tighten but she suppressed her need to complain. David's eyes were directed to Charles. She felt invisible. It was her idea, and he wasn't giving her any credit. In fact, he was criticizing her even as he agreed to do it.

David went on, still talking to Charles. "Remember, we tried it out in a few stores. Gave some designers office space and a desk, and they turned into our best sales reps. We gave them discounts that they passed along to clients. Everyone benefitted. The clients felt like they got a bargain, the designers got more business because they had clients walking in the door. Then, the designers could offer discounts. And we got more sales. And it was all voluntary cooperation. Adam Smith would be proud."

Becca noticed that Charles was silent. She couldn't understand why he wasn't saying anything. Finally, Charles offered, "Yes, that proved to be a stroke of genius."

Becca was annoyed by the flattery. Obvious sucking up.

"So, what store do you want to try it out in?" Again, directed at Charles.

Becca spoke up. "We thought the Deerfield store."

David finally looked over at Becca. "I agree. Why don't you two get started on trying it out there. Carve out a corner and get some merchandise. Let's see how it works."

Later that morning, Becca went to Charles' office to discuss their next steps. "How did you do that?" she started. "We didn't even have to go through the proposal."

Charles smiled. "A wise man once told me to never present anything to an executive unless you already know how they feel about it."

"So, what did you do?"

"I talked with him and felt him out. Tried to see what he would agree to. He didn't want to gamble a couple of million dollars on a concept that we hadn't even tried out."

"I still don't get it."

"I talked with him off and on over the past several weeks. We discussed what we thought *would work*. And I shared drafts of the proposal ahead of time. He actually helped to sharpen the points in the proposal. Then, I appealed to the brand name. If we called it *Architectural Treasures by David Park*, we could leverage our brand equity. Maybe even do some more fun commercials."

"He thought my name of *Becca's Place* was stupid, didn't he?"

"Don't be offended, but it doesn't make good business sense. We've spent years and years developing the brand name *David Park*. To the point where it now means something in the Chicago area. The stores, the ads, and the TV commercials. It only makes sense to try to leverage the brand name."

"Oh, I get it alright. It's all about David. My ideas are only worthwhile if they make him look better."

"It's not like that, Becca. It's good business. Smart business."

"Well, I will show him. I will need a month or so to get some inventory in the Deerfield store. In the meantime, let's clear a section of the floor. Near the front."

"The proposal was to start in the back corner."

"I don't care."

Charles didn't reply. Becca went on. "I will start to get to some estate sales and auctions."

"I would like to go with you."

"Why? Is that David's idea? Doesn't think I can do it?"

"No. It's me. Candidly, I worry that you will overpay for the items, and we won't have the margins to prove the concept."

Becca forced a timid smile. Becca knew he was probably right. Charles was masterful at negotiating with vendors and suppliers. She thought through the sequence. If the business wasn't profitable, then David would blame her for paying too much for the inventory. If

Charles had a say in what they paid for the items, then it would be more likely to be successful. And, if it wasn't, at least David couldn't blame her.

She reached across the desk and squeezed his hand. "You know me, don't you, Charles."

The concept started slowly. *Architectural Treasures* was set up in the rear of the Deerfield showroom, and, weeks after the launch, it had only mustered a few sales.

Becca stood back and scanned the displays. This just *had* to work. It made perfect sense. The displays were impressive. She looked them over. Old doors, vintage lighting fixtures, fireplace mantles, door handles, leaded glass, iron gates, plumbing fixtures, ornate sconces, clawfoot bathtubs.

She wondered how long David would give it before scrubbing the pilot.

Then, they got a big break.

She didn't notice the customer who had walked up behind her. Once the customer said, "Impressive, isn't it?" Becca turned to talk.

It was Cynthia Moriarty. A rehabber who had her own HGTV show, called *Chicago Redone.* Cynthia was a rehabber and designer who would take on renovations. Each weekly show gave updates on her progress on multiple projects. In a few instances, she purchased an old house, renovated it, and resold it. Her show was wildly popular. She stayed with traditional designs and floorplans, and, for many, she brought in architectural salvage, "to give the design some character" she always said.

"Excuse me, aren't you Cynthia Moriarty? From the HGTV series?"

"Guilty. I hope you like the show."

"Yes, it's great. I'm a designer myself."

"Someone told me about this section of the store and I had to come and see it for myself. I just love that old mantel. It would go great in a rehab I am doing in Lincoln Park. And those doors would be perfect for a project I have going in Winnetka."

"Well, let me introduce myself. I am Becca Park. David's wife. I worked with him on developing the whole concept of selling pieces like these."

The two hit it off and Becca found herself giving a tour of the store. Cynthia also "just loved" a well-preserved old clawfoot bathtub. Becca found Cynthia to be just as likable in person as she was on the show.

As she was leaving, Cynthia stopped and said, "I have a wild idea. Would you be open to me having a camera crew come in and film me looking over the architectural salvage and finding items for my projects? You know, act like I am just discovering them?"

Becca's heart raced. She tried to hold in her excitement. "I will have to talk with David, but I am sure that he would welcome the idea."

He did, of course. Both he and Charles saw it as free publicity for the stores.

So, the shoot was scheduled for four weeks later.

David had agreed to have Becca represent the store, and Becca was manic with anticipation. The plan was to have Becca show Cynthia around and let her "discover" the old doors and mantel. Then she would talk about how they would "fit perfectly" with her projects. Becca would offer a little color commentary on how she originally salvaged the items at estate sales. The items were still in the store, but when the episode was aired on HGTV, the episode would show them installed as she envisioned. So, the viewer would see both a "before" and an "after."

The night before the shoot, Becca was lying in bed, staring at the ceiling. She couldn't sleep from the anticipation, and her mind was racing.

Tomorrow she would be front and center. Maybe she would get her own show on HGTV. After all, she had a great eye for design. And for the merchandise. She envisioned a shot of opening credits where she was exploring old, rundown houses and retrieving architectural treasures that she would offer in her stores. There would be upbeat music, with her in action. She would be in skinny blue jeans, with a denim shirt tucked in the front only. She would have to keep the David Park brand name, but she would be running the show. Not David. And she would make sure everyone knew it.

She thought of several episodes where she came in and saved the day when another designer had messed up a project. She would come up with a simple, but elegant, rescue that endured her to her fans. She fantasized about a book deal on spotting hidden treasures. It would probably be on the best-seller list the first week out. She saw it featured on the first table you see when you walk into a Barnes & Noble. Yes, she could become the next Joanna Gaines.

She was very satisfied with the progress of events. Who knew where it could lead?

On the day of the shoot, Becca was positioned at the store and ready to greet Cynthia and the film crew. David and Charles were there, of course. But only for moral support. This was her show.

Once Cynthia and the producer arrived, they asked to talk with her. They went to a more private area.

Matthew, the producer, delivered the news. "Becca, we have given more thought to today's shoot, and we want to change things up a little."

"OK, what do you mean. Do you want me to do something differently? Am I dressed OK? Is there something specific you want me to do?"

Becca watched as Cynthia and Matthew exchanged glances. Then, Matthew said, "We would like to use David himself for the shoot."

Becca's face froze.

Matthew continued, "It's David's name on the store, and we really like how he comes across in his commercials. Folksy, genuine. Like someone's favorite uncle. And he has that deep, baritone voice."

Becca focused her eyes on Cynthia. "I can't believe you are doing this to me."

"We think it is best for the show." Cynthia's eyes did not back down.

Becca couldn't believe that Cynthia, who had seemed so nice, could stab her in the back. She was just like the others.

Chapter 17

Ellicott City, Maryland

Thursday, February 7, 2019

Mellow

Mellow gathered her strength as she eyed the door to the funeral home. She moved slowly, while her Aunt Margie held her elbow. "Stay strong", Margie had whispered as they mounted the steps to the funeral home. Just ahead, she saw her father's body, motionless in the open casket. Mellow secretly hoped that he would just sit up and that this would all be some horrible dream. But it wasn't.

She had been on the Rhine River Cruise when she had gotten the call. From Margie. A heart attack. He had passed quickly. She thought back to the last time she had spoken with him. It had been a few weeks ago. She should have kept in closer contact. Especially after her mother died in 2016. That was from breast cancer, and after a long illness. Once she was diagnosed with the cancer, they retired and moved back to the States. To Ellicott City, Maryland.

Her father's death was much more sudden.

Now she walked into the sitting room with Margie, her last living relative. She approached the casket and it took a short while for her to take in his appearance. He looked so serene. His hair was grayer. His face looked fuller. He still wore his wedding ring.

She didn't notice the size of the crowd at first. It wasn't until she settled into the upholstered chair in the front row. Then she looked around and saw all of the people. It had to be 40 or 50 in all. Who were they? She noticed Aldo, and a few neighbors. But who were all of these others? Near the doorways, she noticed several younger, athletic men with earbuds. Some kind of security staff? For a funeral home?

Aldo was the first to come and offer his sympathies. Then others, many with European accents. Margie nudged her and said, "It's very quiet in here." Mellow then noticed the same thing. Usually mourners visit quietly, but there is always a steady, muffled hum of conversation in the background as people talk with each other. But now she did not hear any background conversation.

After Aldo, another older gentleman introduced himself. James Donovan from the British Consulate. Next came another older gentleman with a German accent. He didn't say his name, but offered that he had worked with her father in Germany.

"I'm sorry, I missed your name?" Mellow asked.

He hesitated and quickly scanned the faces nearby. Then he leaned forward and softly said, "Wilhelm."

This continued for the better part of an hour. Mellow and Margie were both overwhelmed. Beyond his neighbors, almost all were European diplomats. Hungary, Czech Republic, Austria, Italy, France, Poland. Her father had only ever said that he was a "low level administrator who helped Americans in Germany with things like visas, passports, and travel." There were more: Finland, Latvia, Ukraine. Some had traveled from Washington, D.C. Others had come all of the way from Europe.

Mellow remembered her mother's funeral, where the same funeral home had been overflowing with flower arrangements from European embassies. She figured at the time that it was just a polite, diplomatic gesture. Now the Europeans themselves had showed up. On top of the same number of flower arrangements. No, she looked again, there were probably more.

Margie excused herself to get a bottled water. She offered to retrieve one for Mellow, as well, and Mellow agreed.

Once Margie returned, Mellow twisted the cap and, while doing so, recognized a visitor who had just walked in.

She gently grabbed Margie's arm, "Aunt Margie, that's James Baker."

"Who's that?"

"The former Secretary of State under George Bush. The first Bush president."

Margie looked around, and whispered back, "Wow! And isn't that Condoleezza Rice just behind him."

Mellow's eyes widened, "It is. What is going on here? I just can't process this."

Chapter 18

Kinsale, Wisconsin

Friday, February 8, 2019

Mark

Mark was speeding through the main artery of Kinsale when his eyes caught blinking red flashes in his rearview mirror. He checked his speedometer. 50 miles per hour. Seconds later he heard the siren. He looked around but couldn't see any speed limit signs. He didn't really know what the limit was, but figured it was probably 35 or 40.

The squad car pulled up behind him, flashing and blaring. So, he put on his turn signal and pulled into a strip mall. Parking near a 7-Eleven, he sat and waited for the officer to approach. It was taking a while, so he figured that the cop was running his plates. He checked his watch. His dinner reservation was for 6:00. It was already 6:10, and he guessed that Kelli was by now seated and waiting impatiently. She had seemed to be short with him more lately, so he took out his phone and sent her a quick text. *Sorry, running late. Be there in 10.*

Ten was optimistic, given the time that the cop was taking. He put his phone away, since there was no use in letting the cop think that he was using his phone while driving. Best to put it away and have it out of sight. He opened his glove compartment and retrieved the car registration certificate, along with his insurance card. Then, he pulled out his driver's license.

He tried to think about what to tell the cop. Deny that he was speeding? No, that would just make him angry. Tell him he was in a hurry? Probably should. But that might make the cop just go slower in doing what he had to do. He was still thinking through his options when he finally saw the cop approaching. Mark judged him to be in his fifties. Stocky, but fit-looking. A slightly graying mustache.

The cop arrived at Mark's window and said, "License and registration, please."

"Of course." Mark produced both and handed them across, along with his insurance card. "I'm sorry. I know I was going fast. I am very late for an appointment." Mark figured the truth would get the whole ticket process over with quicker. Then he could get to his dinner with Kelli.

"And what kind of appointment is that, Mr. …", the cop pulled Mark's license closer, "Moore. Mr. Moore?"

"Well, it's a dinner appointment."

"With who?"

"My girlfriend."

The cop let out a loud laugh. "That's a great one. A dinner appointment with your girlfriend? Isn't that what they call a *date*?"

"Well, yeah. I guess."

"So, you were speeding because you're late for a date? This is going to be an expensive date for you."

"Well, it's not a regular date. It's a special one."

"And what is so special about it?" The cop's tone had changed from amusement to cynicism.

Mark cleared his throat, and eyed him closely. He decided to stay with the truth. "It's at the Pelican's Catch. I'm going to ask her to marry me." Mark thought that mentioning the name of one of the most expensive restaurants in Kinsale would help his case. It was the kind of restaurant you would take someone for a special occasion.

The cop laughed again. He wasn't buying it.

Mark said, "It's true. Honest."

"So, you are going to propose tonight. He leaned back and folded his arms across his chest. "Then you must have a big fat diamond ring on you. Right? Let me see it."

Mark pointed toward the inside of his sport coat, "It's in my pocket." Mark didn't want to start reaching for things, in case the cop thought he was going for some kind of weapon.

The cop, understanding Mark's pointing, nodded. "Go ahead."

Mark reached into his front pocket and took out the case for the engagement ring. He pulled it up and opened it for the cop to see. "This is it."

"Whoa! That is a monster. Wow."

Mark didn't want to tell him it was 2 carats, and cost nearly $15,000. He checked his watch again.

"Look, officer. Can we just move this along? Can you just write out my ticket? And I will be on my way?"

The cop let out a long breath and took a glance around the parking lot. Mark figured he was thinking through what to do.

Then, the cop looked back to Mark and smiled. "Listen, son. I'm not one to get in the way of true love. I'm going to let you off with a warning, so you can get to this girl and do your business."

"Thank you, officer."

"Just drive carefully, and within the speed limit, as you go." He handed the cards back to Mark. "And, good luck. I hope she says yes."

"Oh, I am sure she will. Thanks again."

Mark pulled out of the parking lot, and was at the Pelican's Catch five minutes later.

The maître d', James, recognized him immediately and said, "Yes, Mr. Moore. Your companion is already seated. Please allow me to seat you. It is at the table you requested."

Mark was well-known at the Pelican's Catch, as were many of the executives from Liffey River Enterprises. It was the perfect high-end restaurant for important business meetings: quiet, a great menu, an impressive wine list, and, perhaps most importantly, allowed guests to linger and talk at the tables as long as they wished. There was never any rush to flip the tables.

Mark had asked for a quiet and secluded table, away from the kitchen and the bar. He wanted the perfect table for his important question.

James signaled the server as he and Mark approached the table, and she hustled over to them.

Mark saw Kelli flick her wrist to check her watch. Then she pulled the loose strands of her blond hair to loop behind her left ear.

He thanked James, and the server stood by as Mark leaned over to kiss Kelli. As he expected, she turned her head and allowed him to peck at her cheek. Kelli was not one for any kind of public display of affection. Mark could tell that she was annoyed with him being late. He figured her demeanor would change as he got to the business of the evening.

As Mark sat down, the server asked, "Can I get you anything to drink while you look over the menu? I will be back in just a minute to explain our specials."

Kelli said, "Just water for me."

Mark ordered a by-the-glass Nickel and Nickel Cabernet.

The server left and Mark said, "I'm sorry I'm late. Got stuck at work. You're not drinking tonight?"

"No, not tonight."

"I tried really hard to get here on time. I drove fast and even got pulled over—".

"Mark, we need to talk."

Mark looked more closely and saw tense and troubled eyes. He sensed that this was something more than him being late.

"I don't want to do this anymore. I am feeling the need to take a bit of a break." Her eyes shifted toward the table.

"OK. I'm not sure I know what that exactly means."

She looked back up and their eyes kept an awkward, uncomfortable contact. "It means I want us to have some time away from each other."

Mark froze. He didn't know what to say. Or think. Should he pull out the ring? Would that change the discussion? No, she was breaking up with him. What happened?

Finally, he said, "I am having a hard time even understanding this. Are you breaking up with me?"

Kelli kept her eye contact. Her face was expressionless. "Yes."

Mark dropped his head. He didn't know what to think. This came out of nowhere. He knew she was getting a little distant with him, but he had figured that was because he hadn't made any moves towards marriage. They had been dating for three years now, and seemed pretty settled on each other. At least to his way of thinking.

He looked at her again. Still no expression. Her eyes vacant. "Is there someone else."

Her face didn't move, "Yes, there is."

Mark let out a deep breath. It seemed so sudden. Disorienting. He put his face in his hands, and said nothing. He couldn't come up with anything to say.

"Who is he?"

"Does it really matter?"

"I did not see this coming."

"Oh my God, Mark." She shook her head slowly back and forth. "You are so oblivious." He heard sadness, not anger, in her voice.

He put his head down again, trying to think through what to do next. He didn't want to create a scene; there were too many people around.

He heard Kelli's chair move and he looked up. She said, "I guess I will go now."

"Yeah, I guess so."

She mumbled a hollow, "Sorry" as she left.

Mark sat alone, trying to sort through what had just happened.

He couldn't make sense of it. Didn't see it coming. If there had been any signs, he had missed them all. Who was the other guy? How long was this going on?

The server appeared with his wine. "Can I take your orders?"

"Just one. Just me tonight. I'll have the seafood salad."

She started to leave, but Mark caught her attention. "And bring me another drink. Bombay Sapphire on the rocks. With a lime. And can you bring my dinner to the bar. I am moving there."

Chapter 19

Barrington, Illinois

Friday, February 8, 2019

Becca

Becca and David were both restless while they waited for their appointment with Dr. Lester Miller. Becca checked her watch. Almost 3:00. Their appointment was for 2:00. This was a follow-up from David's initial neurological exam, and subsequent brain scans.

David's memory issues were getting worse. He had finally agreed to the exam, and they had identified Dr. Miller as one of the best neurologists in the Northwest Suburbs. Perhaps in the entire Chicago area. Becca checked her watch when they were finally called in. 3:05.

Dr. Miller, though in his early-40s, displayed the aura of a seasoned specialist. His words were clear and measured. And he spoke with calm confidence. No wonder he was in such demand. With minimal small talk, he got straight to the point.

"We did the brain scans to try to rule out other causes of the memory problems. The scans showed no hemorrhages, tumors, or strokes. That is good news. The PET scan showed high levels of beta amyloid protein plaques. These plaques are one of the biomarkers of Alzheimer's disease."

He went on to say that, coupled with his neurological assessment, family history, and memory issues, "My diagnosis is that you have an early onset of Alzheimer's Disease."

David let out a breath, "I figured as much. So, what do we do next?"

Becca's mind raced: what does this mean? What should she do now? What happens to the stores?

Dr. Miller replied, "You are still relatively young. You are only 58 years old. And you are in great shape. Your blood pressure is normal, your cholesterol is normal, your PSA is still very low. It is obvious that you get a lot of exercise. All of your lab work is within normal range. You could live for another 30-40 years."

All Becca heard was a jumble of medical words. Her mind left the meeting. What did it mean for her stores? Their social life? Is she going to have years and years of taking him to medical appointments? Oh god, what would her life become? Would she be relegated to being a caregiver for someone who wouldn't even recognize her? Are their finances going to be bled dry with expensive nursing homes?

She caught David looking over at her. He looked surprisingly calm.

Then David turned back to Dr. Miller. "How fast will it progress?"

"It is very hard to say. I can prescribe a medication that will help somewhat. There is some research to show that it can slow down the progression of the disease. It's called a cholinesterase inhibitor. It acts on chemical messengers in the brain, to preserve memory function. This early diagnosis gives you time for planning the services you might need. And to think through what you want to do. It will progress, however, and you will eventually have to consider at-home care, or some sort of residential care. Not right now, obviously. Let's start you on the medication. And come back to see me in a couple of months."

Becca and David were both very quiet as they left the building and walked to their car. Once inside, David said, "You are very quiet."

"I'm sorry. It is just so overwhelming."

"Yes, it is. But it is just something we have to work through."

They returned to silence as they drove to their dinner reservations at the Northwest Grille. Situated in a quiet corner of Deer Park, The Northwest Grille was one of their favorite restaurants. They were recognized immediately and ushered to a prime table.

They each ordered a glass of wine. David a Cabernet blend, Becca a Chardonnay. Becca's mind was still rushing, and she struggled to study the menu. When the server returned with their drinks, she asked to take their order. Becca said, "Oh, I'll just have my usual. Shrimp Alexander."

David ordered a Filet Mignon. 6-ounce. Medium well.

Once the server left, David said, "Honey, I am not surprised by this. I realize that I have been forgetting things. Especially at work. Thank god for Charles being around."

"Yes, this is awful news."

"And I have been thinking about it. For a while." He paused to take a long sip of his wine. "Honey, I have decided to sell the business."

The words hit Becca like a bomb. She scrambled on what to say. "Sell the business? Why do that? Charles could run it. We could keep it."

"No, you heard the doctor. This is progressive. I want to get off of the business treadmill. Even if Charles is running it, I will still worry about it. And I don't want to do that."

"That's a horrible idea!"

"No, it's time. We have always talked about doing more travel. Taking more trips. Now we should do it. We have Italy in May. We should do some more. I want to get back to Hawaii one more time.

Also, South America. We've never been there. And I've always wanted to see Africa. A real safari."

"Sell the business! That's an absolutely horrible idea."

"And we want to get to some of our favorite places in Europe again. Vienna, Zurich, London. And I would love to get to St. Petersburg. We should travel while my memory is still good enough to enjoy it."

"No, you can't sell the business."

David's eyes narrowed on her, and Becca realized that she was pushing back too hard.

"Yes, I can." His tone changed, from entreating to resolute. "I have already talked with a couple of business brokers. We will get a lot of money for the stores."

Becca stewed, but was careful with her protesting. Why wouldn't David talk with her about this ahead of time. She wondered if Charles knew. Did David tell him first?

She felt like David was manipulating her. Told her over dinner in public so she couldn't object or make a scene. He was scheming against her. It was just like the HGTV shoot in the store.

Becca was incensed. But she decided to sit there and just say nothing. She needed to think through what to do. She had to do something. She couldn't lose the stores. And she certainly wasn't going to become a nurse to him.

She gathered herself. "Like you said, this is just something we will have to work through."

Chapter 20

Ellicott City, Maryland

Sunday, February 10, 2019

Mellow

Mellow and her Aunt Margie sat with their coffees in the kitchen of her father's old house. Margie knew where the coffee was kept, and she had prepared the pot before Mellow had arrived. It was time to walk through the house and figure out what to do. Mellow would inherit the house, but she wasn't sure what she wanted to do with it.

"I know this has been all so sudden, but do you think you want to sell the house?" Margie asked.

"I don't know, I am so confused." Mellow took a slow sip of the coffee. "I guess I will sell it. My job is in Europe, after all."

They walked from room to room and took stock of the furniture. "I guess I will end up donating the furniture," Mellow said. "Unless you want any of the pieces."

"No, I'll pass. But I would wait to get rid of the furniture. It is easier to sell a house if it isn't empty."

They arrived in the library. Mellow looked over shelf after shelf of history books. Another section was blocked for fiction. "Pick out any books you want, Margie."

Mellow saw a security camera focused on a door to a closet. "Dad was a stickler for security cameras, wasn't he? He's got them on the front door, the back door, the garage, and a couple more scattered around the house."

She opened the closet door and looked inside. Then she pulled out a couple of boxes and set them on the desk. She took the lid off of the first one and saw several more books. Old paperbacks. Evidently, her father had gone through a Ray Bradbury phase. Underneath the books was another small wooden box. Inside they found several stacks of photos. They covered many years. "Look, it's Mom and Dad at the old Berlin Wall. Looks like around the time it came down. It's dated 1989." She flipped through a stack, while Margie retrieved another. More Berlin. Paris. London. Rome. Vienna. The Jungfraujoch in the Alps. Both of her parents were in most of them. Each dated.

"Oh, I have to keep these, for sure."

Margie stood up quickly, "Oh, I have something for you in my car. I forgot to bring it in. Sit tight." She disappeared.

Mellow looked over another stack of photos while she waited for Margie to return. The second stack had Leipzig, Krakow, Warsaw, Budapest. Mellow thought back to all of the places that her parents had taken her.

Margie returned a few minutes later.

"I'm sorry. I picked this up for you yesterday. Your father had it in the safe deposit box at the bank. He insisted that I have access to it, in case of any kind of emergency. He told me that he had something for you in there. To get it to you if anything ever happened to him."

"What did he mean by *if anything happened to him*? That's an odd thing to say."

"I don't know. He brushed me off whenever I asked about it. But here it is."

Margie handed her a large manila envelope. It was sealed with strapping tape, with "For Melody" written in a black marker. She recognized her father's writing. She felt a slight bulge in the middle.

She struggled to open the envelope, and Margie had to find a pair of scissors in the kitchen to get it open.

Finally successful, Mellow pulled out the contents. On top she found a medal, labeled *Distinguished Intelligence Cross*. A card read, "For a voluntary act or acts of extraordinary heroism involving the acceptance of existing dangers with conspicuous fortitude and exemplary courage."

"Huh, what is this?"

Margie said, "Let me look it up online," and she pulled out her smartphone.

Mellow saw a photo under the medal, "Here's a picture." She examined it. It was a picture of former President George H.W. Bush shaking hands with her father, while handing him the medal. James Baker was also in the photo, but Mellow did not recognize the other people in the photo.

Margie read aloud what she found. "The Distinguished Intelligence Cross is awarded by the Central Intelligence Agency. It is the highest award given by the CIA. It's equivalent to the Medal of Honor."

Mellow dropped the photo to her lap and turned her eyes to Margie. "My dad was CIA?"

The two sat in silence for several moments. Then, Mellow looked at the picture again. "This looks like the early 90s."

Margie went on, "It says here that it is normally awarded posthumously."

Mellow held the picture up for Margie to see. "Well, he was certainly alive for this photo. What did he do to get this? He always said he was just a low-level administrator. But low-level administrators don't get awards like this and don't get their picture taken with the President of the United States and the Secretary of State."

Margie said, "This is amazing. It starts to explain why there were some many diplomats at the funeral home."

"Look, there's more." Mellow pulled out another envelope, also sealed. A sealed envelope inside the larger sealed envelope. Labeled "Melody, Eyes Only."

Mellow opened it. There was a written note that simply read "Stay close to Uncle Aldo. Go to him if you are ever in trouble. You can trust him." There was another photo, this one a grainier black and white one.

Mellow looked it over. It showed a man leaving a building. A street scene. Her father had written at the bottom "Wilhelm Bauer". She pulled it closer to get a better look.

"Who was Wilhelm Bauer?"

Margie, phone in hand, said, "I'll look him up."

Mellow went on, "Wasn't there a "Wilhelm" at the funeral? He only gave me his first name. I remember that because I thought it was strange that he only said his first name."

"I am not finding anything. The only Wilhelm Bauer that is coming up is a Bavarian inventor from the 1800s. He was an engineer who pioneered early German submarines. It says here that the Germans named a U-Boat after him. In World War II."

Mellow held the photo up for Margie. "Does this look like that man that was at the funeral. I know the photo is from many years ago. But it could be him, couldn't it?

Margie focused her eyes on the picture. "Yeah, I suppose it could be him. But this is a very old photo."

Mellow put the photo down and buried her face in her hands, "This is all so overwhelming."

Margie did not reply, but gave her a tender hug.

Chapter 21

Kinsale, Wisconsin

Friday, March 8, 2019

Mark

Mark approached the doorway to his boss's office. Their meeting was set for 10:00 AM. He checked his watch and saw that he was a few minutes early. He leaned his head in. Jerry was on the phone, talking softly with his back to the door. Jerry must have heard him, because he spun around and waved him in, pointing at the chair on the other side of the desk. It sounded like he was in some kind of follow up from last week's off-site meeting.

Jerry was the Vice President of Product Management, and a mainstay at Liffey River Enterprises. They both worked in the Spirits and Wine Division. Sales were less than 20% of the corporations' $7 billion in revenue. It was, as the joke went in the corporation, an afterthought of an afterthought. LRE started out an equipment manufacturing business for the food industry. From there, they grew their own food business, focused initially on private label brands. After a while, they realized they were sending trucks to most grocery stores in the Midwest, and asked the logical question of what else could they put on the trucks. Beer, liquor, and wine seemed like logical candidates. Hence the Wine and Spirts Division was formed.

Mark had asked for the meeting to have a career discussion. He was pretty well-settled on his plan. He had been in his job for the past several years, and wanted more responsibility. He figured he was next in line for Jerry's job. It was well-understood at LRE that Jerry was a few years from retirement. Mark was willing to be patient, but he wanted something else to do, some other challenge that would solidify his selection as Jerry's replacement. From the VP of Product Management role, he would have a direct path to the President of the Division. And he was only 34 years old.

At Mark's performance review discussion, Jerry had begged off of the career discussion. He said he needed more time to see where the new President of the Wine & Spirits Division was at. Bill Langdrum had been hired from the outside several months ago, and people were still just getting to know his style and approach to the business. Mark felt a little more urgency about the career discussion because of the executive changes. Landrum had already replaced the VP of Finance and there were rumors that the VP of Operations was at risk.

Mark heard his phone vibrate and he pulled it from his pocket. It was a text from his mother, Victoria: *Call me when you get a chance. I have a question about Italy.* Their trip to Italy was set for May. This was probably her thirtieth question.

Mark smiled to himself and wrote back: *OK.*

Jerry finished his call and shifted his attention to Mark. After the usual small talk, Jerry began the career discussion. "I've talked with Bill and he has some definite ideas about the business and how to develop executives. He is very impressed with you, and he wanted me to be sure to tell you that. Your presentation on the new wines from Italy were, as he called it, a *home run.*"

"I'm glad to hear that. I think they are working out well."

"As you know, he comes from a Sales background, and he is worried that you have never had a sales job."

Mark knew it was true. He had progressed from market research, to marketing, then a strategy role, and finally, to the Director of Product Management. He gave a noncommittal "mm-hmm."

Jerry continued, "So, he wants you to think about a rotation through a sales role, maybe in one of our regional offices, like Chicago, before he would be comfortable moving you up into a VP level assignment.

Mark groaned inside. This was the last thing he wanted to hear. "Jerry, you know that this is a product driven business. The P&L is driven by products, brands, and low cost of operations. It's not driven by our sales competency. If we have the right brands, at the right price and we deliver on time, sales will take care of itself. Everyone knows that. I can have a much bigger impact on the business in product management than in sales."

"I don't disagree with you, Mark, but he is the President and it is his call. That's the reality."

Mark turned momentarily silent. He could tell that further discussion was pointless. Langdrum was the decision-maker and he wasn't in the room. "Well, alright then. It doesn't sound like I have much of a choice. Doesn't sound like he is going to change his mind."

"No, unlikely. And, you might be surprised at what you see and learn in a sales office."

"So, what's the next step."

"He wants you to meet with Don." Jerry paused, as if waiting for some kind of response from Mark. Hearing none, he went on, "Then, visit the Chicago office and meet with Steve."

Don was the Senior Vice President of Sales, while Steve was the Regional VP of Sales. Mark knew both from leadership meetings and presentations. Don was a gladhander who got along with everyone. He had the gift of gab and always seemed to agree with everyone. Even when he talked with two people who disagreed with each other. Don was the internal candidate for CEO that Bill Langdrum had beat out. Mark was not surprised that the CEO bypassed Don in favor of

Bill. Don just didn't seem to have the gravitas of a CEO.

Steve was probably the best of the Regional VPs of Sales, and obviously the logical successor to Don. And a successor might be needed in the near future, given the dynamics of the hiring of an external President. Bypassed executives rarely make for good direct reports.

Mark understood Bill's approach. His mind spun ahead, and he could foresee that, five or seven years from now, Steve would be the VP of Sales and Mark would be VP of Product Management. The new President was, perhaps, savvier than Mark had thought. He wanted Mark and Steve to get together and form a close relationship.

Mark's mind wandered, but just briefly. He wondered why he could see things so clearly in business and business relationships, but not in his personal life. It had been exactly one month since Kelli rejected him, and he still could not figure out how he hadn't seen it ahead of time. He still felt blindsided. Now he wondered why he was thinking about his personal life during this important career discussion. It made no sense.

He forced his attention back to Jerry. "Should I just call Don?"

"No, let me reach out to him first, and let him know you will be setting up some time. Bill wanted me to feel you out on this before we pulled Don into the discussion."

Mark left his boss's office and began to think through his approach to Don. What questions to ask. How eager he should look. What questions Don will ask.

Back in his office, he cleared out a dozen emails. Then he called Victoria.

She started with, "Mark, I am just not getting this washcloth thing. What kind of hotels are we staying at if they don't even supply towels and washcloths.?"

Mark smiled to himself. He had tried to explain it several times. "They have towels, but many European hotels don't provide washcloths. So, just to be on the safe side, you need to pack a couple. You may not even need them. This is just to be cautious."

Victoria had never been to Europe, or even left the country for that matter. Mark's father had always said that they would take a European vacation once he retired, but his heart attack and subsequent death came only weeks after his retirement party. Mark told his mother that he would take her, and he set up the Kastner Tour to do so. He knew Italy well, from his prior business trips to Tuscany and Umbria.

"Yeah, sure. Mark, I also want to talk about this whole dating thing. I know that Kelli hurt you badly. But, if you fall off the bike, you need to just get back on and start riding again."

Mark was silent for several seconds.

Victoria filled the gap. "You need to get back out there again."

"Mom, I am not having this conversation with you again. I am not talking with you about my dating life."

"Well, the right girl is out there for you. But you can't stop looking."

It was clear that the question on washcloths was a ruse for her to make her dating pitch. Yet again. "I need to run. Do you have anything else about the Italy trip?"

"No, I'm good. Love you."

Chapter 22

Barrington, Illinois

Sunday, April 14, 2019

Becca

Becca stood in her Great Room and took stock of her plan. She glanced at the clock on the bookshelf and saw that it was a few minutes after 11:00. David was off with his biking friends. He said they were going riding in the forest preserve and would be back after 11:00. That would leave him time to shower, eat a quick lunch, and then get to their Barrington store ahead of the 1:00 opening.

She surveyed the layout. The shelves were to her right, while straight ahead was a wooden coffee table, positioned centrally on a rug that covered most of the hardwood floor of the sitting area. A sofa and two chairs were positioned around the table. They had decorated the shelves with a few framed photos, as well as other small items they had secured on their travels. Most important for her plan was a small glass pen holder. It was hand-blown glass, about the size of a baseball, with a single slot for a pen. Designed for a desk, Becca and Charles loved the blue and white swirls, and used it instead for decoration in the Great Room. They had bought it from a very talented artist in Sedona, one who went much beyond the junky crystals and jewelry that seemed to populate the stores. Neither Becca nor David bought into the goofy idea of *energy vortexes*, but they had to admit that some of the artwork was terrific.

She went over and picked it up. Bouncing it in her hand, it felt heavy enough for her plan. When he came home, she would wait for a moment when he was not looking. She would hit him hard with the glass ball. Right on the corner of his forehead. On the left side, hard enough to knock him out. He wouldn't see it coming and so she would be able to get a good swing at him. Then she would drag him over to the wooden coffee table, and bang his head on the corner of the table. She would make sure it was the same spot she hit him with the glass ball. She would have to bang his head down hard enough to do real damage. She wanted to go well beyond him just losing consciousness. She would have to make sure his skull cracked. It might take several tries. And she would have to make sure it is in the same spot on his forehead, so the coroner didn't get any ideas about it being anything other than a weird accident.

Then she would bunch up the rug near the coffee table so that it looked like he tripped and struck his head. She would put the glass ball back on the shelf. Fingerprints didn't matter, since it was her pen holder anyway.

She put the glass ball back, grabbed her phone, and went out on the patio to wait. Just in case any neighbors were around, she would wait there. When she heard him get back, she would jump up and act like she just heard a noise. Then rush into the house. Just in case any neighbors saw her. The busybodies to the left always seemed to be watching her. She would use that to her advantage.

Her story will be that she was on the patio and heard a bang. She rushed in and found him passed out. He must have tripped over the rug and hit his head on the corner of the coffee table. When the ambulance came, she would have to do her best to be upset.

Now she just had to sit on the patio and wait. She felt

surprisingly calm about the whole situation. After all, it wasn't her fault. This is what she had to do. She had no choice. What was she supposed to do? She certainly was not going to be a caretaker for him. Like the doctor said, he could live another 30 or 40 years. Was she supposed to put her life on hold? And then David says he is adamant about selling the business. And, after all, he was the one who insisted on the prenup. The stores were in an LLC that he controlled, and the prenup stipulated that, if they divorced, she would get nothing. If he preceded her in death, she would get the LLC, meaning the stores. Then, she would have Charles run it for her. He would then be free to divorce his useless wife, Sharon.

Becca thought back to how her affair with Charles had started. She remembered the exact location. They were at an old farmhouse in McHenry County. Becca was distraught over a second HGTV shoot in which she again was pushed to the background. She vented to Charles, in an old barn, and then began to softly cry. Charles offered a sympathetic hug, which became a longer embrace, which became prolonged eye contact, which became a tighter embrace, which became a passionate kiss. It was magical, and Becca knew then that they had to be together.

So, really, she reasoned, this is all David's doing. He ignored her desires to be in the HGTV shoot. He is the one who insisted on the prenup. And he certainly couldn't expect her to be his nursemaid for the next 40 years.

She checked the time on her watch. Nearly 11:30 now. He was late. Maybe they talked him into stopping for coffee. No, he would have called.

Her mind returned to her plan. She told herself again that this was on David not her. What did he expect? Ignoring her. Disrespecting her. Pushing her into Charles' arms. Selling the stores. She was only doing what she had to do. In just a short while, this would be over, and she would then be freed up to marry Charles.

With an airtight prenup, of course.

Her phone rang. It was Scott, one of David's biking friends.

"Becca, I am calling from an ambulance. David fell off his bike and got banged up pretty good. He is conscious, but his knee is really banged up, and it looks like he hurt some ribs too. He is in a lot of pain."

"What? How did this happen?"

"He hit a rut and went off the trail. His knee went straight into a large boulder. We are on our way to Good Shepherd."

"OK, I am leaving now. I will meet you there."

Chapter 23

Zurich, Switzerland

Tuesday, April 16, 2019

Mellow

Mellow was just about to crack open her newest Donna Leon mystery. She wondered what adventures were in store for *Commissario* Brunetti. She had a few days before her next Rhine River Cruise, and she was looking forward to the downtime. A good mystery, and some quiet time, would be wonderful. She had finished her dinner, homemade turkey soup, and was settled into her living room chair. She had Strauss waltzes playing softly on Pandora. "Tales From the Vienna Woods" was just starting. She had a glass of Brunello already poured. It was going to be a delightful evening.

Her iPhone rang and she checked the caller ID. It was a German number that she did not recognize. She shrugged and answered anyway. Probably work-related.

"This is Melody." She used her real name instead of "Mellow" because others found "This is Mellow" to be rather awkward.

"I understand that you have been looking for me." It was a

man's voice. Speaking English, but a German accent.

"Who is this?"

"This is Wilhelm."

Mellow straightened up in her chair. "Wilhelm?" She grabbed the remote and paused the music. The book fell closed on her lap.

"You have been making a lot of phone calls to find out about me."

Mellow hesitated, unsure of what to say. She had indeed made several calls to the U.S. Embassy in Berlin, and the Consulates in Dusseldorf and Munich. She had also called the U.S. Embassy in Zurich. And the German Federal Foreign Office in Berlin. No one had any information on anyone named Wilhelm Bauer. No one had ever heard of him. She had even called Aldo, who also offered no information.

Collecting her thoughts, Mellow said, "First of all, thank you for coming to my father's funeral. That was very much appreciated. I am just trying to figure out who you are. And what you have to do with my father. He had never talked about you."

There was a pause on the end of the line. Then, Wilhelm said, "Your father was a great man. But there is nothing I can tell you about him."

"You must have been close to him. You went all of the way to the U.S. for his funeral. I am just trying to fill in some gaps."

"I wish I could help you. But I cannot. You do need to stop making inquiries."

Mellow picked up a seriousness to his very last sentence. His tone sounded almost ominous. He wasn't threatening; it felt more like a friendly warning.

"What do you mean by that?"

Again, a pause. Wilhelm was measuring his words. "It is dangerous for you to be asking about me. I wish I could tell you more, but I cannot."

"Why can't you?"

"I am going to hang up now. Please just let this go."

"Wait a minute!" Mellow couldn't let him just hang up. She struggled with what to say next. Finally, she asked, "Is that really you in the photo? You look much younger in it."

Wilhelm did not hang up. After several seconds of silence, he asked, "You have a photo?"

"Yes, I do."

"I must have that photo. And any copies you have made of it."

"I haven't made any copies." Technically, that was true. Mellow did not make any copies with a copy machine. But she did use her iPhone to snap a photo of the photo. Just to make sure she had a backup.

"Please describe the photo."

"It's a photo of a man, you at a younger age I am guessing, coming out of a building. In a business suit. You are not posing, so it looks like you didn't know your picture was being taken."

"Anything else?"

"My father wrote 'Wilhelm Bauer' on the bottom of the photo. And he wrote several numbers on the bottom of the photo." Mellow still hadn't been able to figure out what the numbers represented. Not a phone number. Too long for an address. Not a postal code.

"What numbers?"

"I think I have said enough. If you want the photo, you need to tell me about my father."

Again, a long pause. "Alright then."

"I'm listening."

"We'll meet for coffee tomorrow. In the morning. Bring the photo. Once you give it to me, I will tell you about your father."

Mellow's mood brightened. Finally, she would get some answers. "Where do you want to meet?"

"There is a coffee shop a few blocks from your apartment. Henrici's. I will be there at 10:00. Bring the photo."

Then the line went silent.

Henrici's was a great choice. Busy. Great coffee. Very popular with locals. And it was only three blocks from her apartment. But, how did Wilhelm know where she lived? Or her cell phone number, for that matter? She felt vulnerable. She had been trying to track down Wilhelm, but he knew more about her than she did about him.

She thought she better call Aldo. So, she scrolled through her phone until she found his listing. She was about to call him, but then stopped. Aldo would tell her not to meet him. Tell her she would only be disappointed. Or just tell her again to just let it go. She had told him about the photo, and he had dismissed it, saying "It's probably just some leftover photo from his embassy days." He would press her on why she felt a need to meet Wilhelm. Or, worse, tell her that he wanted to be there. Then, Wilhelm would probably clam up. Or just leave.

No, she would just go by herself and meet with Wilhelm. Maybe she would tell Aldo later. He would probably just get in the way now.

It worried her that Wilhelm told her it was dangerous for her to try to track him down. But she had to learn more about her father. CIA? And so many European diplomats at the funeral? The Distinguished Intelligence Cross? Photo with President Bush? Maybe Wilhelm could provide the answers.

She put her book away. She was in no mood to start a murder mystery.

She arrived the next day at Henrici's well ahead of time. She wanted to get a good inside table, one where she could watch people coming in and out of the door.

There was a buzz of activity at the outdoor tables, and Mellow liked the energy of the place. She had been there many times before. Inside, she got her *caffe crema* and secured a spot at one of the wooden tables. She hung her red leather crossbody bag over the corner of the chair and draped her jacket over the back of the chair. Just to make sure, she peeked inside the bag and confirmed that she had the envelope with Wilhelm's photo. She watched the bustle of people coming in and ordering, sitting at a table or taking their drinks to an outside table. Many bought the pastries or quiches.

From her seat, she had a direct view of the front door. She would be able to spot Wilhelm well before he actually entered.

She pulled out her iPhone and checked for emails and texts. A few from work, but nothing that demanded her immediate attention. So, she put her iPhone back in her bag, pulled the zipper closed, and then turned her eyes back to the door. She wasn't sure what she would learn from Wilhelm. But she might get some answers about her father.

She waited several minutes. More patrons came and went. No Wilhelm yet.

Then she heard a commotion outside. A couple was arguing. Loudly. A server went out to check on them. They got louder. The activity grabbed the attention of several other customers. These sorts of disturbances just didn't happen in Switzerland. Some of the customers walked quickly past Mellow to look out the window. Now the man was raising his voice again and pushing his chair away from his table. Mellow leaned forward to get a better look. What is wrong with him? She couldn't see very well, so she got up and stood beside her table. More customers went past her. Then, as quickly as it started, the man and woman walked off. The server returned and told her co-worker at the counter, "Must have been some kind of lover's spat." They both laughed. The counter clerk's wisps of purple hair shook while she laughed.

Mellow sat back down and took a drink of her coffee. Still more coming and going.

But no Wilhelm.

So, she sat and waited. By 10:20 she finished her coffee and realized that he would be a no-show.

She stood to leave and grabbed her jacket from the back of the chair. She looked down in horror. Her purse was gone.

The blood drained from her head. She felt faint, and so she sat back down. This was a complete disaster. Her keys. Her iPhone. Her passport. Work badges. Credit cards. Bank cards. Cash.

She quickly stood back up and started to scan the crowd, looking for anyone or anything that might be suspicious. She hustled to the counter and grabbed the attention of the purple-haired server. "Someone just took my purse."

"Oh no!". The clerk shouted to gain the attention of the café manager. She came over right away, a serious-looking woman in her 40s.

"Let's look around. Many times, they just take the cash and throw the purse aside. They don't want to be caught with it. They can always claim the cash was theirs."

Mellow agreed. She usually did not carry much cash. She probably only had 40 or so Euros, and even less in Swiss Francs.

The manager went to the back exit, through the kitchen, while Mellow went outside. She even opened up the trash receptacle and peered in from the top. Nothing. She walked a few shops down, first one direction, then the other. Nothing.

She was angry with herself. As a tour director, she had always warned tourists about crime and how not to make yourself an easy target. Now *she* was the victim.

But she had done everything right. She had a crossbody bag that hung over her shoulder and kept her arms free. It had slash-resistant straps, with thin strands of steel. RFID blocking pockets to protect her cards and passport. Lockable zippers. And she had put it under her jacket.

All she had done was to stand up and lean over to check on the disturbance outside. But that was enough. She realized that it had all been a distraction, so that her purse could be stolen.

She let out a resigned sigh and started to walk back to Henrici's. And she began to think about how complicated it would be to get everything back. Her work situation was a complicated combination of passports, residence permits, and work permits. She was only able to secure it all through the efforts of Kastner Tours.

Literally, she only had the clothes on her back. No key to her apartment. No cash. No credit cards. No identification. And she was due to start a River Cruise in Germany in a few days.

This was a complete disaster.

The manager was waiting for her when she returned. "I'm sorry. I have not been able to find anything. But I have called the police. They should be here any minute."

"Don't you have some security cameras?"

"We do, but they aren't working right now. I noticed that this morning before I opened. They were fine yesterday. I called the security company, and they said they could send someone this afternoon."

Mellow did not know what to say or do next.

The manager said, "Can I get you another *caffe crema* while you wait?"

Mellow hesitated, and the manager quickly added, "There will no charge, of course. I am very sorry this happened. We never have these kinds of things happen here."

"Thank you."

Mellow was barely back at her table with her new coffee before two officers arrived. With typical Swiss efficiency, they gathered the necessary facts and were on their way. They were sympathetic, but they did not offer much optimism about Mellow ever seeing her bag again. Or the contents in it.

So, she finished her coffee and walked back to her apartment. She buzzed the landlord's apartment, and Mrs. Widmer quickly came over the speaker. Mellow, embarrassed, explained that she needed help getting into her apartment because her purse had been stolen. Mrs. Widmer shouted, "Oh you poor thing!" She buzzed her in right away, and then greeted her just inside the door. They walked together up to the third floor while Mellow recounted the events.

Just as they approached the top of the steps, Mellow looked ahead toward her apartment.

She saw her crossover bag leaning against the door to her apartment. The red leather was unmistakable, and a wave of hope rushed over her.

She ran ahead and picked it up. Just inside she found a note. She also saw her keys, her phone, her ID cards, her bank cards, and her credit cards. The envelope with Wilhelm's photo was missing. All of her cash was still there.

She opened the note. It was printed, very neatly, in English.

Ms. O'Neal,

I just wanted the photo. I cannot let you keep it. I have also deleted the photo from your camera roll. I wish you no harm. Please stop pursuing me. There is nothing I can tell you about your father.

Wilhelm

She scrolled through her photos. The one she had taken of the photo of Wilhelm was indeed missing. She checked her call logs: the call from Wilhelm was missing from her *Recents* list.

She thought about her iCloud files. She had decided many years ago not to pay the additional fees to have all of her data backed up on an iCloud drive. She had blown through the free storage within months of getting her phone, and her phone had not been backed up for years.

She thought back to her father insisting that she never send or store any personal information on the internet. "Never. Never. Never," he had demanded. She agreed, only because he was so adamant about it. She also had to promise that she would never get a Facebook account. "Never. Never. Never."

Bypassing Facebook was easy for her. She had seen what people posted on it and decided that it was a complete waste of time. To say nothing about surrendering her privacy.

Bidding goodbye to Mrs. Widmer, who seemed as relieved as Mellow, she went into her apartment and locked the door behind her.

She leaned against the back of the door and again looked at her iPhone. She figured that, even if she had the photo backed up on her iCloud drive, Wilhelm would have erased it from there as well. Just like he hacked and disabled the security cameras at Henrici's.

Now the original photo was gone. The picture she had snapped was gone. She would never be able to figure out what the numbers meant. Or who her father really was.

Chapter 24

Barrington, Illinois

Wednesday, April 17, 2019

Becca

Becca pulled into the Barrington Walgreen's parking lot. She had gotten a text that her prescriptions were ready. There were two. Hers was Clonazepam, her anxiety drug for the flights to and from Italy. David's was oxycodone, for pain from his knee surgery.

His biking accident had done serious damage to his right knee. He needed major reconstructive surgery. Fortunately, his ribs were just bruised, not broken. But they hurt as well. His surgery was Monday, two days ago. He was home now, and Becca had gone out to pick up his pain pills.

Walking into the Walgreen's, she looked up and noticed the security camera. They seemed to be everywhere these days. She envisioned some low-paid, but eager, security team watching her every move. She made sure not to look directly at the camera.

Inside, pharmacist Kate gave her several words of caution about the oxycodone. "It's an opioid and can get addictive. Be very careful, especially in mixing it with other drugs. And no alcohol."

Kate had filled her Clonazepam before, and, as before, alerted her about the dangers in combining it with alcohol.

Becca thanked her and, again avoiding the cameras on the ceiling, made her way out.

Once back home, she found David where she had left him. He was stretched out on the Great Room sofa, knee elevated on pillows. Remote in hand, he was surfing channels trying to find something to watch.

"Oh my god, Becca. There is absolutely nothing to watch during the day."

"Yeah, maybe try Netflix. If you want, we can do another episode of *The Crown.*

"Maybe after lunch."

She went to the kitchen and got him a glass of water for his pain pill.

"The pharmacist said you can't have any alcohol with these."

"Yeah, yeah, yeah. That's what the doctor said too." He waved it off. "A little scotch is always good medicine."

"Don't forget your exercises. Here is the sheet from the physical therapist." She handed him a stapled packet of papers.

"Yeah, I need to do those. I have to get back to walking if we are going to keep our Italy trip."

"We can change it if you want."

"No, let's go. I will be strong enough by then. We need the break."

Becca returned to the kitchen and pulled out the product information sheets. She was familiar with her Clonazepam. There was no need to read it. But the oxycodone was new. She studied it in detail.

She found the warnings to be pretty menacing. "OxyContin is an opioid agonist and a Schedule II controlled substance with an abuse liability similar to morphine."

She read on, passages that said it can cause drowsiness and

sleepiness. Not to mix with alcohol and not to mix with any other prescription drugs without your doctor's approval. Respiratory depression is the chief hazard for oxycodone, including coma and, possibly, death.

One particular paragraph caught her eye.

> Patients should not combine this drug with alcohol or other central nervous system depressants (sleep aids, tranquilizers) except by the orders of the prescribing physician, because dangerous additive effects may occur, resulting in serious injury or death.

She put the sheets down and looked over at David. Then she turned her head and stared out of the kitchen window. A germ of an idea was forming in her mind.

Using the blue and white pen holder, along with the corner of the coffee table, was now out of the question. David was not mobile enough, and he was too deliberate in his steps, to have anyone believe that he would trip; he needed assistance and careful watching.

Her new idea was starting to crystallize. But she would have to do more research.

The next morning, she got David situated in the Great Room and told him she had to go out and run some errands. He nodded OK without even appearing to listen. He didn't even look away from his Jason Bourne movie.

She left her phone at home. On purpose, so no one could do any GPS tracking of her.

She drove the 12 miles to Schaumburg and found her way to the Main Library. Spotting the outside security camera, she was careful to not look up. There was no need to look suspicious. She was sure that they were watching her, and she didn't want them to know that she knew that.

Likewise, when she got to the top of the steps to the second floor and walked over to the computer area, she avoided any direct looks at the cameras.

She asked to use a computer, only to learn that she needed a Schaumburg Library Card. She explained that she only had a Barrington Card. The very helpful clerk, a Millennial named Monica, accepted it and sent her to the bank of computers. "Feel free to use whatever one you like."

There were only a few patrons in the area, and she sat at a computer that positioned her back to the windows. That way, she could see anyone who might walk past her and see what was on her screen.

She opened a browser window and went to the library website. After a little searching, she found the pages about their privacy and security policies.

Reading on, she found out that her assumptions were true. For reasons of privacy, the library did not monitor or track the websites that users accessed. After each usage, the history cache was deleted. There would be no way for anyone to find out what websites she investigated. On top of that, the clerk had not recorded which computer she was using.

It was perfect. By not using her iPhone or home computer, no one would be able to, later on, go through her browsing history and see what she had been researching. And by using the Schaumburg Library instead of the Barrington Library, she would not be appearing in any Barrington security footage. Even some ambitious or determined detective wouldn't think to check the cameras of all of the neighboring libraries.

She opened a new window on the computer and went to Google News. That way she would have a second window open already in case someone walked by and saw her screen. She could quickly toggle to the Google News window.

She smiled inside at how clever she was.

Finally satisfied, she went to the original window and began her searches.

Within an hour she learned a lot.

It was very dangerous to mix Clonazepam with oxycodone. Coma, and death could occur. One study suggested it could occur as quickly as within 30 minutes. With alcohol, things would be even worse.

Alzheimer's patients quite often lose track of when, or if, they have taken their prescriptions.

Oxycodone can become very addictive. And people can habituate to it, needing even higher doses to get the same pain-killing effect. It is twice as potent as morphine.

She also found out a lot about the U.S. State Department. It offers assistance to U.S. travelers in cases of death while in Italy. And, the U.S. Embassy was only a mile or so from the Rome hotel in which they would be staying.

Italy, like the U.S. has seen a surge of opioid overdoses. She could expect the Italian hospitals to be familiar with patients who overdose.

Autopsies are normally required in Italy. Death certificates are required before the body of a deceased U.S. citizen could be shipped back to the U.S.

It would take 5-7 days to get the body back to the U.S.

The State Department "stands willing" to assist with any situations involving death of a citizen while on vacation. How convenient.

Having completed her queries, she closed out the windows on her screen. Then she turned off the computer. She switched it back on and looked up the internet history. Nothing.

Smiling, she gathered her things and left. She kept her head down as she walked past the eyes on the ceiling.

Chapter 25

Kinsale, Wisconsin

Tuesday, April 23, 2019

Mark

Mark had a hard time focusing at the Business Update meeting. This was the typical monthly update that offered the routine agenda of reports from Sales, Distribution, Operations, and Marketing. Since it was April, Finance gave a report of the First Quarter performance. The LRE earnings report would be in less than two weeks, and the numbers were taking final form. Results were solid, but not great.

He was bored by it all. It seemed to be the same people basically saying the same things each month. He found himself scrolling through his emails. After he finished his scan of the emails, he found his mind wandering to his upcoming trip to Italy. He had been there several times on business. Florence, Tuscany, Umbria, and Venice. Unfortunately, he did not have time, or, truth be told, take the time to see much of the sights. This trip would be different. It would be 10 days across most of the key things to see and do in Sorrento, the

Amalfi Coast, Rome, Assisi, Florence, and Venice. He pictured himself casually browsing through small wine shops, talking with the locals, and trying out new wines. And new foods. It would be great.

His daydream was interrupted when his boss, Jerry, asked for a word or two about the rollout of the Umbria project. The project involved newly imported wines from Italy. Their price points were perfect; between the super cheap wines from South America and the overpriced Napa offerings. Mark had done the blind taste testing between the Umbria and Tuscan wines; consumers actually preferred the Umbria reds. People paid up to be able to say that their wines were from Tuscany. Just like Napa wines weren't any better than the Columbia River wines of Washington State, but people paid up just to be able to say that their wine was from Napa. And the popularity of Mark's new wines was showing up in the business results. Overall sales in Wine and Spirits were flat, but the new wines from Italy, along with his recent French imports, were making up for declines in the liquors.

Mark knew the presentation by heart: it had been his baby for the past several years. He explained that the next leg of the strategy would be a new label, from the Columbia River Region of Washington. They would position the new wines like they had the Umbria ones, but this time they would be adding a new label that would be for restaurants only. If that worked, they would go back to Umbria and do the same.

The meeting ended and he walked back to his office. The red light on his phone was blinking: new voice messages. He was glad he had checked his emails during the meeting. At least he didn't have those to pound through as well.

After entering his voice mail password, he heard, from Joyce the Voice, "You have … four new messages". He started through them.

First was a request for a copy of a research study on the Umbria tasting panels. The second one was from Paul Blanchard at Harris & Blanchard, a boutique search firm that was focused on consumer businesses. He recognized their name, but had never talked with any of their headhunters. He listened to the other two messages. One was a vendor calling to request a meeting, to find out "what keeps you up at night." Oh brother. The fourth was from HR, asking to reschedule a candidate interview.

He sent out the research report, and then called HR to discuss the schedule change.

With time before the end of the day, he decided to call the executive recruiter.

So, he called Paul Blanchard.

He connected quickly, which surprised him. He had been expecting a game of phone-tag, where he and Paul would exchange voice messages for a couple of days.

"Mark, thank you for returning my call. I have an opportunity to discuss with you. Can I explain it to you?"

"I'm not really looking. I am very happy here at LRE."

"Well, please indulge me for ten minutes. Maybe you know of someone that might be interested."

"OK, go ahead."

So, Paul explained the position.

Mark was intrigued by it.

The following Saturday Mark found himself sitting across from Paul at the Chicago office of Harris & Blanchard. It was only a four-hour drive. He had left Kinsale at 6:00 AM, and was comfortably seated by 10:30. Since it was a Saturday, the drive was a breeze. And downtown Chicago was empty. The office was at 111 East Wacker, just off the corner of Wacker and Michigan Ave. He took the elevator to the 19th floor. Paul's office was on the northwest corner, with a great view of the city. Paul pointed out the landmarks. Looking down, he could see the Chicago River and the top of the new Apple Store.

Paul told him about the Apple Store on the other side of the river. "They had quite an issue with the pigeons right after it was built. For all of their planning, they had a major issue with pigeons, and pigeon droppings when they first built it. It was hilarious. Each morning you could see workers cleaning off the pigeon droppings."

They both laughed about it.

Paul pointed out the Tribune Tower, Trump Plaza, and North Michigan Avenue, with the Water Tower straight up the street.

Then Paul began the conversation, "Let me start by recapping what I explained on the phone earlier this week. Our client is a private equity concern that owns a substantial player in the wine distribution business. They are in the Baltimore area. They were formed by a couple of former vice presidents at T. Rowe Price. We think this could be a great opportunity for you."

After more discussion, Paul asked Mark for his thoughts on the role.

"Their strategy looks interesting. And they want to go public in a few years?"

"Yes, that, or a SPAC. They believe that the industry, while it has some major players, is ripe for a rollup strategy. They want to acquire some other east coast players and become a major force on the east coast. Then, a few years later, go public and then move into other US regions; South, Midwest, and then the West coast. Their timeline is three years to go public, then, within five or seven years, become one of the top three distributors in the U.S. You would be the obvious CEO. Who knows, they could be buying the Wine and Spirits division of Liffey River Enterprises?"

Paul's comment was clearly not meant to be threatening, and Mark did not take it as such. Still, he knew that the Wine and Spirits Division was not the main business of LRE, and it was quite possible that LRE might, down the road, sell them.

He knew that, while he might aspire to become President and GM of the Wine and Spirits Division, he would never be considered for CEO of LRE.

"Would this require a relocation to Baltimore?"

"Yes. At least initially. Once they go public and start their expansion to other regions, the Headquarters could be anywhere. If you were the CEO, I'm sure they would be open to a move to the

Midwest. By that time, they will only be shareholders. They would not be involved in the actual running of the business. They will be moving on to other things."

"Can I ask why me? I am flattered, but wouldn't they want someone who is already a President or GM? Or someone with experience in mergers and acquisitions?"

"They have plenty of M&A expertise already. They know what they are doing in that regard. They asked us to survey the industry to see who would be the key industry leaders in the next five to seven years. When we did that, your name kept coming up."

"I see." Mark felt flattered, and he was surprised. But he did his best to act like he wasn't. Better to be seen as confident and self-assured, he figured. Better to act like someone who expected to be a President or CEO in 7 years.

"And then when we shared your name, they said that, and I will quote. 'We definitely want to talk with him, he's the guy kicking our butts with his Umbria wines.' So, here we are."

Mark laughed, "Yes, we are having a lot of success with those wines."

"It turns out they tried a similar strategy a couple of years ago. But it didn't work out."

"Yeah, we included their wines in our tasting panels research. I have a good sense of why their wines didn't work. They tried vineyards from the Piedmont region, which is more expensive. With higher expenses, they were too close to the Tuscan price points. And their wines were too fruity and acidic. I am guessing they used the opinions of wine experts, instead of real consumer research."

Paul smiled. "Yeah, they will want to meet you."

John V. Noonan

PART THREE

John V. Noonan

Chapter 26

Rome

Wednesday, May 22, 2019

Mellow

Mellow awoke from the gentle shaking by Gina. Her phone alarm was ringing. She reached onto the nightstand and turned it off. 7:00.

Gina had slept on the pullout sofa in the sitting room. She put it back together and came back to see Mellow.

"How are you today?"

"Much better. I think the sleep did me good." Her head was throbbing, and her left knee was now swollen even more. Still, she replied, "I think it has passed and I will be fine. Thank you so much for staying here."

"My pleasure. Dad says you are like family, and you know what that means to an old Italian like him." She laughed out loud.

There was a knock on the door.

"I ordered a light breakfast for you. That must be it."

It was, and Gina left. Minutes later, the room phone rang. She gimped her way to the phone.

"*Pronto*".

"*Boungiorno.* Well, you must be better if you are answering the phone like an Italian." It was Aldo.

"Yes, I am much better. *Grazie.* I think I am almost back to normal."

"Just checking. Let me know if you need anything."

"*Grazie.* And tell Gina she is the best."

Mellow found her way to a mirror. She took off the bandage that the ice man put on last night. She saw a large yellow and red bruise on her forehead. It took several minutes to cover it with makeup.

She looked again at her knee. Swollen, but she could walk, still hobbling a bit but faster than last night.

She still had a headache, but it was more of a dull throb, not the piercing stabs she felt last night. She took two more Tylenol with her breakfast of expresso, a bowl of fruit, and a small pastry.

She figured that Angelo would somehow let Luca know about her fall. She sent Luca a text: *Had a minor stumble last night at the Spanish Steps. A little stiff, but I am fine. Just wanted to let you know. Nothing to worry about.*

Then she sent Angelo a text: *Thanks for your help last night. I am much much better this morning. Meet at coach at 8:30? Guests at 8:45.*

He wrote back: *Glad you are better. See you at 8:30.*

Chapter 27

Rome

Wednesday, May 22, 2019

Becca

Becca and David walked through the *Rilassante* doors and started toward the Kastner coach. Becca was stunned to see Mellow greeting guests at the door of the coach. She came to a complete stop, and David asked, "What's the matter?"

"Oh, nothing." Then she continued on.

She approached Mellow. "I am so sorry to hear of your fall." She could see a bruise underneath the makeup on Mellow's forehead. "We heard about it at breakfast this morning"

David chimed in as well, "You know, you said yourself that they were tricky to navigate. Glad you are back at it today."

"*Grazie.*"

Becca and David checked the new seating chart on the inside of the door and found their way to their seats. It took longer to board everyone, as each had to express their sympathies to Mellow.

Once all were settled, Mellow took to the PA.

"Thank you all for your kind words this morning. I am feeling a lot better. We have a very busy morning. We are going to start with a driving tour of the main tourist area. I want you all to try to get a mental map in your mind of how the various sites are laid out in relation to each other. Please take out the map I left on everyone's seat. We are going to go roughly clockwise. We will start at the Spanish Steps. Appropriately so."

The group gave a polite chuckle.

"Then we will go past the main train station. Then on to the *Piazza Venezia*, where I will point out several points of interest. Then a quick drive up the Capitoline Hill, and then back on our circular path toward the Vatican. On the last leg, I will point out how to get to the *Pantheon* and the *Piazza Navona*."

The coach pulled away. Becca looked out the window. She was only half-listening to Mellow. She couldn't believe that Mellow was still here. She was certain that even a minor injury would have resulted in Mellow being pulled from the tour. All that she needed was a few days. David would be dead, and she would leave the tour before Mellow even got back. She wondered if Mellow saw her on the Steps. Probably not. But someone else might have. She had scanned for the security cameras and only found a few. She figured there had to be more.

The coach took a right turn, and Mellow announced. "Look out to your left. You'll see the Spanish Steps, named after the Spanish Embassy that used to be at the bottom of the steps. We are on the *Piazza di Spagna*. Built in early 1700s and restored several times since. It's a popular meeting spot for both locals and tourists. There are always a couple thousand people here. It's also a great spot for people watching, and, like I said before, there are fantastic views from the top. Especially at night."

Becca's thoughts returned to her dilemma. She was not going to let Mellow ruin her plans. She had to figure out a way to get rid of her. Evidently, a small-scale injury wasn't enough. She would have to do more. Well, if she needed to, she needed to. And she would do it.

Mellow continued her droning on about Rome. She was so annoying. "Coming up straight ahead is the main train station. This has about 800 trains coming or going every day, with about 450,000 passengers each day."

Mellow kept talking, but Becca was elsewhere. She wondered who else Mellow told about seeing her and Charles in Amalfi. She knew that Mellow told that local guide. And Angelo too. She could tell by how Mellow and Angelo were always looking at her. She probably told a bunch of other people too. She is just a gossip. Someone who enjoys sticking her nose in other people's business. She just looks like the type.

"Now we are at the *Piazza Venezia*, which is one of the most noteworthy spots in Rome. Angelo is going to pull to the side for just a bit. Up on the hill is a large structure that looks like a wedding cake. This is the memorial to Victor Emmanuel, who was the first king of Italy when it was united in 1871."

Becca looked out the window, up at the columned monument. Yes, she would have to get rid of Mellow. And not be so nice about it this time. She didn't feel sorry for her at all. She had to stick her nose where it didn't belong. She is getting what she deserves. Just like David. Healthy as a horse. Gets Alzheimer's. He could live another 25 or 30 years. He shouldn't expect her to take care of him forever. He'll just bleed the money dry. Forget that. Not when Charles was the one she was meant to be with. Yes, she needed a plan for Mellow, just like she came up with a plan for David. And fast.

"Now look to the right of the *piazza*, and you'll see a shorter three-story building with a balcony hanging out in the middle of the second floor. See it there? That is known as Mussolini's Window. That is the balcony he used to give speeches to his followers. Picture this *piazza* in the 1930's, with a hundred thousand people crowded together and Mussolini giving a passionate and heated speech from the balcony. I am not exaggerating. If you do a search online, you will find photos of him at the balcony with throngs of people listening."

Becca was hoping that Mellow would just shut up so she could think. *David wants to sell the stores and retire. Instead of letting her and Charles run them. He won't listen to reason about it either. Pigheaded. He's already talked with the lawyers about looking for buyers. And he will start that in earnest once we get back. Can't let him do that. He deserves what she has in store for him. He made her sign the pre-nuptial agreement. Whatever she does, it's really his fault. What else* could *she do?*

"We are going up the Capitoline Hill. On your left is a long set of steps going up to the *Piazza del Campidoglio*, which was designed by Michelangelo in the early 1500s. He also designed the three buildings at the top. Today these house museums. In the center of the square is a statue of, guess who, my favorite emperor, Marcus Aurelius. Take a look at the steps. Yet another set of Italian steps that you have to be very careful on. These were designed by Michelangelo himself."

Becca looked at the steps but her mind was elsewhere. *How could she do it? She needed to think of something quick.*

Something as clever as what she was doing with David. The opioids were a godsend. Especially since he has Alzheimer's. Really, who is going to question anything if an Alzheimer's patient loses track of his pills and takes too many. It was perfect. He forgets, goes looking for more, finds her Clonazepam, and takes it instead of his own pills. And she has already set the stage with him arguing with her about whether or not he took his pills. In front of witnesses. So what if they find too much oxycodone and some Clonazepam in his system? He did it to himself. There would be witnesses to her trying to give him the correct doses.

"Now we are back on our clockwise route. On our way to the Vatican. To your right, only a block or so, will be the *Pantheon* and about three blocks to the west of that will be the *Piazza Navona*. We will be stopping to see them tomorrow. The *Pantheon* dates back to the year 120 and started out as a pagan temple. It became a Catholic church in 608 and has been in continual use as one since then. That is why it is the best preserved of all of the old Roman structures. And the *Piazza Navona* is probably the most famous of all of Rome's piazzas. It houses three fountains, including Bernini's famous *Fountain of the Four Rivers.*"

Becca wasn't even looking or listening anymore. And there is no way to trace anything back to her. There were absolutely no tracks for anyone to use to trace things back to her. She had seen enough *CSI* episodes to know the tricks the investigators use.

She felt a nudge from David. "What are you smiling about? You are staring off into space with the weirdest smile on your face."

"Oh, nothing. Just enjoying the tour. Just thinking how Rome is so great."

Mellow saved her from any further explanation. "Now we are pulling up to St. Peter's Square and the Vatican."

Chapter 28

Rome

Wednesday, May 22, 2019

Mellow

Mellow checked her watch. They were a few minutes early. She saw a tall man waiting at the designated spot near the Vatican and figured it was the local guide, Giuseppe Russo. She had called him while they were on the coach, and he described himself as tall and said that he would be wearing a light blue dress shirt, white trousers, and brown shoes. Had to be him.

She announced that they were pulling up. "Before we get off, I noticed that no one said anything about my scarf today. Guess you are all getting used to them. But this one is special. Note the colors. Red, blue, yellow, and orange. Anyone want to guess why I have this one on today?"

No one offered. "Today you will see the Swiss Guard in their very colorful uniforms. And the colors are ... red, blue, yellow, and orange."

She got a few laughs, and one, "Oh that's cute."

"And again, I want to remind you that the Vatican expects a level of reverence while you are in the Vatican. Please talk softly and remember where you are. Do not be surprised if you see the guards remove people from the line if they are not dressed appropriately, or from the Basilica itself if they are not behaving appropriately. They take dress and decorum very seriously. To many of them, this is the holiest place on the planet. Now, sit tight for a minute while I check in with our guide, Giuseppe."

She stepped off and greeted Giuseppe. They exchanged pleasantries. He was very tall, probably six-three or six-four. Not thin, but not overweight. Looked like a rugby player who just cleaned up.

"Here is the Whispers microphone. The on-off switch—"

"I know how to use it. I've been doing this a while. No need for an explanation. Can we get going?" He clipped the microphone onto his shirt.

Mellow heard annoyance in his voice. He was terse and abrupt. She did not push it. Old Mellow would have reacted quickly to his abruptness and gruffness. But New Mellow just let it go.

"Sure, let me get them off the coach and introduce you."

It took only a few minutes for the group to exit the coach and bunch around Mellow and Giuseppe.

Giuseppe took over right away. "*Buongiorno* everyone. I am Giuseppe. Let's get together in the ellipse. Follow me."

Mellow hung near the back of the pack to make sure she didn't lose anyone. Plus, it helped with her knee, which was still stiff.

Once at the ellipse, Giuseppe began, "We are in St. Peter's Square. Or, in Italian, *Piazza San Pietro*. There are two sections before we go into the Basilica. We are at the ellipse. The section ahead of us is squarish, just before the doors to the Basilica." He then went through the basics of the Square. 284 columns that are 4-deep. Ellipse is 320 meters by 240 meters. 140 statues of saints at the top of the columns. Mellow thought that his delivery was very mechanical.

He moved the group up about 50 feet. "The Apostolic Palace is the building behind this set of columns. On the top floor, the second window from the right is where Pope Frankie comes out each Sunday to pray with the crowd in the Square."

There was a round of laughter from Giuseppe using the phrase "Pope Frankie." He smiled and seemed to enjoy the reaction.

"Now let's go forward a bit. Look straight ahead at the Basilica. The window with the red curtains is the balcony Pope Frankie uses when he comes out to give blessings or speeches to the crowds in the Square."

They moved some more, and stopped again. "And can anyone guess where we are standing now?"

No one talked. But, Giuseppe did not give them much time to respond.

"This marker here on the pavement, I believe you are standing on it, young lady, marks the exact spot Pope Paul II was shot, in 1981."

Victoria looked down and realized she was the one standing on the marker. She let out one of her loud laughs and said, "Oh, I'm sorry!"

"The Pope recovered. A Turkish assassin was captured and served many years in prison. After he was released, he asked Pope Frankie if he could see him. Needless to say, Frankie said no."

"The Basilica holds 20,000 to 30,000 worshippers. The *Piazza* will hold 300,000. In 2014, at least half a million people attended the ceremony to canonize Pope John XXIII and Pope John Paul II. I call them Pope Johnny and Pope JP2."

Giuseppe seemed to again enjoy the laughter from the group. He pointed out the long line waiting to get into the Basilica. "Those people are going to wait about an hour and half to get in, but we are going to get in right away through a separate entrance. Wait here for just a moment."

Mellow walked ahead with him and, after a very brief conversation with the Swiss Guard, the group began to file into the Basilica. They went through the security checkpoint with ease.

Once inside they moved directly to Michelangelo's *Pieta*. Mellow was always amazed that such a famous sculpture was just inside the doors. Of course, it was behind bulletproof glass.

Giuseppe made a few comments—from a single piece of Carrara marble, in pyramidal form, and it is the only piece he ever signed—and then moved up the aisle. Again, it felt very mechanical to Mellow.

Giuseppe went on. "Now that you are inside you can really appreciate the size of the Basilica. It is the length of two football fields and the width of two football fields. The interior is the height of a thirteen-story building." He paused for effect, and the guests swiveled and arched their necks to see it all.

He pointed toward the artwork on the walls, "Now, you can take pictures inside the Basilica because, believe it or not, those are all mosaics, not paintings."

"And be on the lookout. You never know when Pope Frankie might appear. If he does come out, don't go sneezing to try to trick him into a blessing. Frankie doesn't like that."

Victoria let out one of her louds laughs, and Mellow winced. Way too loud for the Vatican. People from other groups looked over at them.

Giuseppe spun and glared at Victoria. "We told you about keeping your voice down in the Basilica. You Americans come over here and just think you can do anything. The way they enforce behavior is that they ban any guides whose groups don't behave."

He wiggled his index finger in her face. "You Americans go back home on a plane. I stay here. You are affecting my livelihood. What is wrong with you, anyway?"

Victoria froze, and her face reddened. Mellow saw Mark striding up toward Giuseppe, daggers in his eyes. She hustled forward, despite her aching knee, and stepped in front of him, "Mark, I will handle this."

Mark stared at her for several seconds, then relaxed his shoulders and said, "OK."

She spun toward Giuseppe and yanked the clipped microphone from his shirt. Then she pulled off the Whispers transmitter that was attached to his belt. "Thank you, Giuseppe. That will be all. We won't be needing you anymore today. I will take over the narration." Then she bore a hole in his eyes. Everything seemed to get quiet. No one was moving. Mellow could tell that all eyes were on her and Giuseppe.

Mellow sensed that Giuseppe wanted to say something, but, instead, he let out a long breath and walked away.

"OK, then. Let's move on." She clipped the microphone to her blouse and held the transmitter in her hand. "We are going to walk down toward the main altar. The canopy you see over the altar is called the Baldachin. It was sculpted in bronze by Bernini in the early 1600s. Each of the four columns are over 60 feet high. And it was designed to fill the space pointing up to the cupola."

Mellow then finished off the tour of the Basilica. She knew she was taking a big risk. She was not a licensed guide in Rome. Or any other Italian city for that matter. Or the Vatican. But she had to intervene. And she had to finish the tour of the inside.

So, she did. She showed them the mosaics up close, pointed out the features of the inside of the dome, and walked them back toward the front to see the tomb of Pope John XIII. She always thought his tomb was especially interesting, creepy at that. Inside a sealed glass case, the embalmed body of Pope John XIII was visible for all to see. Face and all. Remarkably preserved.

Then, Mellow couldn't help herself. She took the group back to the *Pieta*. "I want to point out a few things that you didn't hear when we stopped the first time. First off, Michelangelo was only 24 years old when he created the Pieta. And it rocked the world at the time because it was a natural form that helped to define the Renaissance, not an idealized form. Second, take a close look at Mary. She must have been at least 50 when Jesus was crucified, but here Michelangelo portrays her as much younger. Almost the same age as Jesus. Art historians have offered a lot of hypotheses about why he did that.

But we will never really know."

After pointing out the *Navicella* mosaic above the entrance, which Giuseppe had also missed, Mellow led the group out the doors. They walked through the ellipse toward the coach, which Angelo had parked along the main street leading to the Square.

As they approached the coach, Mellow saw Giuseppe walking toward her. She slowed to let the guests move on and board the bus. Mark must have seen him too, because he slowed his walk as well. He motioned Victoria to continue toward the coach. He took a position only a few steps away from Mellow. Not close enough to participate, but close enough to hear what they would say.

"Mark, you don't need to stay. I got this."

"No, I am staying." She saw a seriousness in his eyes that she hadn't seen before. He was still doing a burn about how Giuseppe had talked to his mother.

Giuseppe began his attack even as he approached Mellow. "Let me straighten you out. You are *not* a licensed guide and I should report you. I don't want any of this nonsense tomorrow at the Colosseum." He stood over her, at least a foot taller.

"We won't be needing you tomorrow. You are done with this group."

"Well, I am going to report you. You are probably going to act like a local guide tomorrow, too. Aren't you? That's illegal."

Mellow took a quick stock of her situation. Someone had pushed her down the Steps. Her head still hurt. Her knee was stiff. Her relationship with her driver was strained. Her boss basically said she would be fired if anything went wrong on the tour. She caught a couple having an affair on the tour. She was not a licensed guide and Kastner could get in trouble if Giuseppe pushed it. She had tried to be the New Mellow and let things slide.

But she was at her limit. She had tired of tiptoeing around everyone.

She bent her neck back to look up at Giuseppe and she put a pointed finger in his face, inches from his nose. "Listen, Sparky. I will not have you barking at my guests. You can report me to anyone you want. I don't care. But if you do anything, I will call the Commander of the Swiss Guard and tell them that you are referring to Pope Frances as Pope Frankie. And that you also use names like Pope Johnny and Pope JP2. So, if you want to take me on, then be my guest."

She turned and walked to the coach, not even looking back.

Striding past Mark, she said, "C'mon, Mark. Let's go."

Mark hustled to catch up to her, then walked with her. He snickered, "Well that was impressive."

Angelo was waiting as they got to the door of the coach. As they approached, Angelo said, "Mark, please get on the coach. I need to talk with Mellow for a minute."

Mellow was thinking: now what?

Mark stepped onto the coach, and Angelo walked Mellow several steps away.

Angelo began, "I heard from the guests what happened. I can't believe the guide talked about our Pope Francis like that. If I had heard it, there would have been fireworks. I don't go for that kind of disrespect. And talking to a guest like that. I am proud of you for standing up and taking over. Melanie and I have never used him. I may talk to him myself tomorrow."

"We won't be seeing him tomorrow. I fired him. Looks like I need to find a replacement."

"Do you have the authority to fire him?"

"No." She gave him a slight smile. "But I did anyway."

Angelo laughed out loud. Then he said, "If you don't find anyone, I can do it. I know Rome as well as any of these guides."

"Are you licensed?"

"No, but I know the story as well as any of the local guides and no *Polizia* in Rome is going to bother me. Most of them know me."

Mellow replied, "Well we may have to do that."

Angelo put his head down. "I owe you an apology. I have not treated you well on this tour. But it makes me very proud as a

Catholic that you defended our Pope Francis. And I am proud that you would stand up for our guests like that. If you need anything else on this tour, you just let me know and I will get it done."

Mellow felt genuinely touched. "Thank you, Angelo." She took a few steps back toward the coach, then stopped. "We have to do something for the guests to make up for this. What do you think about another nighttime tour? This time the Colosseum? I know we are going there in the morning, but it is quite a sight to see it lit up at night. And Trevi and the Vatican last night was very well received. I am thinking just a drive around. Maybe stop for just a few minutes for some pictures."

"I think they would like that a lot."

"OK. Done."

They went back onto the coach and Mellow took to the PA system. "Thank you for your patience and understanding. The behavior of our local guide was inexcusable. I apologize for that. We won't be using him anymore. And Angelo and I have come up with another fun activity for tonight."

She described the evening drive to the Colosseum, and she walked the aisle to take the names of those who planned to go. All signed up except the Parks and the Collins.

Finishing, she went back to the PA. "We have 14 going tonight. Let's meet in the lobby at 9:00. It will be very dark by then. We should be back by 10 or so. And then tomorrow we will go back for the formal tour. Then we'll visit the *Pantheon* and the *Piazza Navona*."

She settled into her seat and Angelo started off. Now, what to do about Giuseppe? She took out her iPhone. She remembered her father always telling her that when there was conflict at work, "the first one to the boss usually wins". He had said that if she was ever in a conflict at work, then it was better for the boss to hear of it from her instead of whoever she was arguing with. She wished she had done that with the last river tour. Maybe Luca wouldn't be so quick to discipline her. Then again, she smiled to herself, if she went to Luca whenever she had a conflict, she would be texting or calling him every other day.

Still, she decided that this time she would take her father's advice. She sent Luca a text: *Had an incident this morning. Local guide did not work out. I think it is minor, but want you to know about it. Can you talk this afternoon?*

She smiled again. The "minor" was a hedge. A spin.

He wrote back right away: *In planning meetings all day, can I call you tonight? At 7?*

Yes, that works.

After they arrived at the *Rilassante*, Mark hung back to talk with her. Mellow had a small group of the guests visiting with her outside the coach. They offered thanks and support. The consensus? She had done the right thing. They were looking forward to the Colosseum trip tonight. Last night at the Trevi Fountain and St. Peter's Square was truly magical. Even with the crowds at Trevi.

Finally, it was just her and Mark. He said, "Thank you for stepping in. It was a good thing you did, because I was about to launch on him."

Mellow wasn't sure what he meant. She imagined for a brief moment that Mark, dad-bod and all, would actually start a physical fight with the hulking Giuseppe. After all, he had basically attacked Mark's mother. She kind of admired that. "Well, I am not familiar with the phrase *to launch* but I can't have a guide talking to a guest like that."

"I didn't mean I would have hit him, but it would have been a loud and nasty exchange. We all probably would have been thrown out."

"Yeah, we couldn't have that."

Chapter 29

Rome

Wednesday, May 22, 2019

Becca

Becca settled into the sofa in the lobby of the *Rilassante*. David was asleep back in the room, and she needed some time to think through her next steps. The Vatican tour had tired him out, and, after two days of extra pills, David was fatigued. Last night in bed he was struggling to breathe. After he fell asleep, he was almost panting, like a runner who had just finished a quick dash. Becca thought he might just pass away during the night. But that would have been one day too early. Tonight would be the night. She pulled out her pill container and doublechecked the slot for Wednesday. There it was, one of her Clonazepams. Almost the same color and size as his pain pill. Her plan was brilliant. And it would work.

She rehearsed the steps in her mind. She had her Clonazepam in his pill container. He would probably order a drink, wine most likely, at the group dinner. He shouldn't have alcohol with either his pain pill or the Clonazepam. But he would. He wouldn't be able to help himself. Then, he would ask for his pain pill. She would object, enough that others would hear. He would argue, and she, after acting as the concerned wife, would give him her Clonazepam, the anxiety reducer that would interact with his pain pills and the alcohol. He would pass during the night, if not sooner.

Then, she would call the hotel and ask for a doctor. An ambulance would take him to a hospital.

The tour group would move on without her. Charles and Sharon would obviously stay to support the grieving widow.

The ultimate resolution would be that it would be declared a tragic case of an Alzheimer's patient accidentally taking an overdose of an opioid, along with too much alcohol.

If, by chance, they did additional testing and found the Clonazepam in his system, then she would say that he probably took it, mistakenly, from her pill container when he was trying get at his pain pills and sneak an extra one. The containers were nearly identical.

She had thought of everything.

She would stay in Rome for a few more days, and then she would fly back to the U.S. with David in the cargo hold.

Then she would be free.

But there was one wrinkle that had come up. Mellow. She would blab about seeing Becca and Charles. Then, things might unravel. She couldn't let that happen.

She would have to deal with Mellow as well. And she already had a plan for that.

She checked her watch. It read 2:30. She had a couple more hours before the group dinner. There were no planned group activities for the afternoon. It was free time for the guests to explore Rome on their own. Mellow had given them a handout of ideas. Some *piazzas*, some tourist sites, but mostly encouraging them to take the time to just wander the city.

She left the hotel and headed south, away from the *Via Condotti*. She would have preferred the expensive shops, but they had a lot of security cameras. She didn't want to be on any. Plus, she just needed a cheap, but heavy, tourist souvenir. So, she went in the direction of Trevi Fountain. With all of the tourists in that area, she would surely find something to fit her needs. She pulled up the map on her iPhone.

On every sidewalk, and at every intersection, she walked through a mass of people. It was like Midtown Manhattan at rush hour. Cars were everywhere, and motorcycles and scooters jumped in and out of the traffic. None of the streets were straight and perpendicular. She had to check her iPhone map repeatedly to stay on course. It took her over fifteen minutes.

Near Trevi, as expected, she found a cluster of street vendors. It was a collection of junky, cheap tourist gifts: pendants, postcards, small statues of St. Peter's Dome and the Colosseum, fake leather, scarves, wall hangings, busts, pens, jewelry, earrings, photos, crosses, vials of Holy Water, and painted cups, plates, and bowls. She stopped and surveyed the throng. She thought to herself *Oh my God, I am in Hell.*

But people were actually buying the junk. She edged her way to one vendor who had tables jammed with merchandise. She had to wait for another tourist who was trying to decide upon her purchase.

The heavyset, older tourist said, "I am looking for some holy water". Then she turned and nodded toward her female companion, also older and overweight.

The vendor said, "Right over here, *signora*." He pointed further down the table and the two women moved down, allowing Becca to slide in next to them. Then, he held up a small white plastic container, emblazoned with a cross.

"Is it blessed, or is it just water?"

"*Signora*, I only sell real Holy Water." He signaled with his finger for them to come closer. "And I will tell you something," he looked both ways then back to the woman, "These bottles have been blessed by Papa Francesco himself."

"Who is that?"

"Pope Francis. You see I have a cousin who works at the Vatican. I am the only one of all of these tables that sells them."

The two women looked at each other, "No way!"

The woman beamed, "Then I will take three of them. How much are they?"

"I normally sell them for 10 euros, but because I can see that you are a good and religious person, I will sell them to you for 8 euros."

"That's terrific. Thank you."

The vendor pocketed the money and the two women, giddy with their luck, marched off.

The vendor looked at Becca. "Yes, *signora*."

Becca turned her eyes back at the junk on the table. "I am looking for a small statue. Something like a paperweight."

He picked up a large statue of Michelangelo's David. "We have this one. Only 50 euros."

"No, that's too big."

He looked over his table, then picked up a smaller version of the Colosseum and handed it to Becca. "25 euros."

Becca bounced it in her hand. Too hard to grip and still too big.

"No, maybe something even a little smaller." She picked up a small bust. Heavy and easy to grab onto. "Something like this. Who is this?"

"Who were you looking for?"

"I don't know, maybe an emperor. Julius Caesar?"

"Well, that is who you have in your hand. You are lucky today."

Becca twisted her hand and looked it over. "How much is this one?"

"That is a fine piece. Genuine bronze. 30 euros."

Becca knew it wasn't bronze. But it was heavy enough and it fit well in her hand.

"I will give you 10 euros."

"20." The vendor gave her a smile that did not match his cunning eyes.

"I will do 15, but no more."

"That will do, *signora*."

Becca paid in cash and he placed it in a paper bag. She did not want a receipt.

"I can tell that this is not your first time in Rome, *signora*." The vendor then switched his attention to the tourist standing beside Becca, "*Buongiorno, signora*".

Becca stepped away and again checked her iPhone map. She figured that, since she came this far, she may as well go on to actually see Trevi Fountain.

She was disappointed. There were thousands of tourists and she couldn't get anywhere near it. She looked over the top of some heads and saw the upper portion. But she couldn't even get close enough to take a photo.

So, she headed back to the hotel. As she approached, she looked up at the security cameras. Feeling like she didn't want to call attention to herself, she quickly looked away.

Once inside, she headed to the lower level. The steps were just past the elevators. The *Rilassante* was a boutique hotel that catered to tourists. Still, they had small conference rooms for the occasional business meeting or reception. They were all downstairs. Two at the bottom of the stairs and a larger one down the hallway. She looked toward the ceiling and could not see any security camera. She walked into the first room. It was set up for a business meeting: a large oval table with 12 chairs around it. A few additional ones were placed haphazardly against the walls. No, this one wouldn't do.

She checked on the second room. It was the same size as the first, maybe 40 by 40. But it was much more inviting. A small table and chairs were set up at the back of the room. Three sofas, maybe 15 feet inside of the door, were near the front, bracketing three sides of a large wooden coffee table. No window. No camera. She felt the hard edge of the table. And the corner came to a sharp point.

It was perfect. Even better, it had a single door that closed for privacy. With a lock on the inside. Yes, this one would do.

Just to be thorough, she checked out the larger room at the end of the hallway. It was set up with six table rounds. No tablecloths. And the chairs were stacked against the far wall.

Leaving, she saw an easel in the hallway, still lettered with the events from yesterday.

There clearly wouldn't be anything going on in these rooms for a while.

Everything was coming together quite nicely.

Chapter 30

Rome

Wednesday, May 22, 2019

Mark

Mark and Victoria approached the Spanish Steps, and Mark declared that Mellow had it right. This was a mass of humanity. Thousands of people, locals and tourists alike, scurried in each direction. Some up the Steps. Some down. Many, too many, just sitting wherever. Some old, some young, a wide variety of clothes and colors. The bright sun forced many to squint, as if in a permanent clench of their face. Gelato in cups appeared to be the catch of the day. Mark was expecting it to be noisy, and it was, all of the voices projecting a boisterous background.

Victoria "just adored" the azaleas that framed the Steps, two vertical lines that marked the way to the top. Victoria was exuberant, "And just smell those things! This is just amazing!"

Mark was adjusting to the crowds in Rome, and so he plowed ahead. They stopped near the fountain at the foot of the Steps and saw that it would take a while to navigate their way forward. So, they pressed up the first few steps, Mark charting a path around the squatters on the lower steps.

Mark heard his phone and checked it. His boss, Jerry.

"Mom, it's my boss. I need to take this. Must be important."

She made a face and announced, "Well, I am going to go ahead. Meet me at that first lookout."

"I will be there as soon as I can."

He heard a dismissive "yeah, sure" as Victoria was already walking away.

"Hi, Jerry." Mark moved away from the Steps to try to find a quieter spot.

"Mark, I don't want to bother you on vacation, but I have some news that I think you will like. When you get back, Don wants to meet with you to talk about the specifics of moving into the Chicago Sales job."

"OK, that's good."

"It's a short stint, maybe 18 months. They just want you to be there long enough to experience the seasonality of the business. Then you will be set up for a promotion to an executive, VP assignment."

Mark's phone vibrated in his hand, and he pulled it away to check. The caller ID showed that it was Paul Blanchard, the recruiter from Harris & Blanchard. Mark wanted to switch over, but he couldn't hang up on Jerry.

Mark gave a half-hearted, "Great. Looking forward to it." He let Paul's call go to voice mail.

"This will be a great move for your career. By the way, what is all of that noise in the background."

"Oh, I am outside. At the Spanish Steps. It's pretty crowded. Rome has people everywhere."

"Well, I will let you get back to it. Enjoy the rest of your vacation. And Don will meet with you when you get back. I think this will be a great move for you."

After the call ended, Mark peeked back at the Steps. He couldn't see Victoria, but figured she was well on her way to the first lookout.

He called Paul Blanchard back, and Paul picked up right away.

"Mark, I have fantastic news! They want to move forward with an offer. Brad is going to call you to present it."

Brad Nichols was the Managing Partner at the private equity group, and the key decision-maker that interviewed Mark. "That's great." This time he did not have to feign enthusiasm.

"It will have a substantial increase to your base salary, a higher incentive target, and the details about equity and stock once they go public. Obviously, he is the one who wants to give you the specifics. He just wanted me to make sure you would be available. He knows you are in Italy".

Mark reflected back to the interview. At the time, he could tell that the interview was going extremely well, because, halfway through, the buying and selling switched. Typically, when an interview starts, both sides are checking each other out, but the reality is that the hiring manager is in the driver's seat. At the start, the candidate is selling and the company is buying. Once the hiring manager starts selling, which is what Brad had switched to, it is a really good sign.

Mark thought momentarily about what Victoria's reaction would be. He had told her about the possibility of the Chicago job. It was only three hours away and very drivable. Plus, it was imminent.

Baltimore was a different story. It was a couple hour flight from Kinsale, Wisconsin, and 13 or 14 hours by car. And there had been no assurances that he would get the job. So he had not told her about it.

She would be disappointed in his moving away, but she would understand. It would mean financial independence. He would be the President of a good-sized business, and, down the road, could be the CEO of a much larger one.

There was no doubt in his mind that he would be successful, and the venture would succeed. They had excellent capital backing, and a strong business strategy. And he knew that he had the smarts, and the drive, to pull it off.

"This is great news, Paul. I am looking forward to the call. What time is he thinking?"

"8:00 your time, in Italy. 2:00 his time."

"That will work."

"Oh, and be sure to be available. You know from the interview that he is a stickler on time. And he is pretty impatient. He would not look kindly if you end up playing phone tag with him.

"I understand. I will make sure that I can take his call."

"I will get back to him and tell him that you will be sure to be available."

Paul congratulated him again and they ended the call.

Mark knew that the departure time for the evening drive was 9:00. He figured that the timing would work out well. At 8:00, he would be in his own room, and Victoria would be in hers. He could easily take the call.

He couldn't believe it. He was going to be the president of the business. And then a CEO.

He looked up the Spanish Steps, scanning for Victoria. The crowd made it very difficult. But then he spotted her. Waving wildly at him from the railing at the first lookout. She cupped her hands and seemed to try to shout. Yeah, like he would be able to hear her.

If anyone was playing "Spot the American", here was one for sure.

Chapter 31

Rome

Wednesday, May 22, 2019

Mellow

Mellow arrived at *Ristorante Verucchi's* at 5:00, ahead of the 5:30 start time for the *Aperitivo* for her group. Angelica and her staff were setting up. Arranging tables and chairs, doing final wipe-downs, and organizing the buffet.

She tracked down Angelica. "*Buona sera*, Angelica." They gave each other air kisses.

"It is so good to see you again, Mellow. I assume you want to go over the menu. Let's go back to the kitchen." She stopped momentarily. "I love the scarf, by the way."

"*Grazie*. I wear it for my Vatican trips. The colors match the Swiss Guard."

It was the same Angelica; pleasant while still focusing on business.

Angelica led her through the dining area and into the kitchen. Then she handed Mellow a menu for the evening. The top read

"*Benvenuto*! For Our Special Kastner Guests!" Listed below were the dishes for the event, in English of course. Angelica began to review them, as Mellow followed along.

An impressive assortment of cheeses. Deep fried artichokes. Cured meats. A variety of pizza slices. Vegetables. Samples of pasta dishes from their menu. Seafood bites. Small salads. Various breads. And a separate table for a dessert buffet, with all sorts of surprises. Including four or five flavors of gelato.

It was exactly what Mellow had asked for. "This looks perfect! I know it is a heavy menu for your *Aperitivo*, but this will be their meal for the evening."

Angelica nodded. "And, as you expect, we have a full bar. With Campari, of course." She turned the menu over to show the list of drinks.

Mellow expected the Campari, a bitter liquor that was a staple of an Italian *Aperitivo*. Mixed with gin and vermouth, and paired with an orange slice, it formed the classic Negroni, the standard for an *Aperitivo*.

"I very much doubt that you will need it. These are Americans, so they will probably be drinking wine and martinis. Some will have beer. It is all I can do to get them to even try a limoncello." They both laughed.

The guests started to trickle in just before 5:30. Susan Allen and Charlotte Johnson, the Pharmacy sisters from North Carolina, arrived first. James and Keisha Jackson were just behind them. All four settled into a table near the bar.

Mellow went over to greet them. "*Benvenuto*! *Benvenuto*! Welcome to your first *Aperitivo*. I trust you all had a fun afternoon."

Keisha replied, "We did. We walked over to the Villa Borghese. It wasn't that far. And you were right, it is spectacular. And so big. We didn't have time to cover much of it. We didn't get to the gallery. We just walked the grounds."

Mellow was not surprised. To do justice to the Villa Borghese would take a full day in itself. "I am glad you enjoyed it. Maybe on your next trip you can do more."

She turned to Susan and Charlotte. "And how did you two ladies do?"

They both proudly thrust out their necks, each loosely tied with a colorful scarf. "Notice anything?"

"I see. They are gorgeous."

"I know you said that Florence was a place to buy scarves," Susan said. "But we saw these and couldn't resist. I love it, because it makes me feel dressed up."

Charlotte added, "Yeah, we asked ourselves, "What would Mellow do?" And we decided that you would buy them. So we did! We can get more in Florence!" The sisters laughed; Susan a reserved chuckle, but Charlotte a boisterous guffaw.

The other guests had arrived while Mellow was talking, so she quickly excused herself to greet the others. They were all pretty much on time. She smiled to herself. Her harping about being on time was paying dividends.

The Parks had arrived with Charles and Sharon Collins. Mellow had watched them walk in and David looked to be struggling to walk. He took a seat at the first available table and let out a long breath once he settled into his chair. He did not look well. Mellow went over to check on them all. "How are we doing? Did you get around at all this afternoon?"

David was the first to respond. "No, I took a nap. Becca had to go out wandering by herself."

"Yeah, I walked to Trevi Fountain. But it was so jammed I could barely see anything."

Charles and Sharon walked to the Spanish Steps. "All the way to the top," Sharon proudly declared.

Mellow scanned the room and saw that all were there. "Well, excuse me, I am going to start the proceedings."

She called the group to attention and reviewed the plans while she distributed the menus. "We have the restaurant to ourselves until 7:00. We are going to experience a real Italian *Aperitivo*. Think of it as the old American Happy Hour, but with really good Italian food instead of fried American barfood. More like heavy hors d'oeuvres."

She saw that she was getting blank stares.

"You'll see. Their regular *Aperitivo* starts at 7:30, when they will open to the public. They have kindly opened up early for us. The food is already out, so help yourselves to the buffet. And I encourage you to try everything. The drink menu is on the back side of your sheet. Order whatever drink you like. I recommend that you try the Negroni. It is a classic, and, if you have one, you will experience a real *Aperitivo*. The food menu is pretty heavy for an *Aperitivo*, but I told them that this would probably be your meal for the evening. So, Buon Appetito!"

The food was a great success. But, as expected, most drink orders were wine and martinis. So, Mellow ordered several Negroni's and had them split into very small tasting glasses. She carried them around to the tables and encouraged them to try it. Most did, finding it too bitter and too strong. They went back to their wine and beer.

Oh well, she had tried. Marsha and Monica both said that they planned on a limoncello at the end. That was some progress.

Everyone was enjoying the food. And the drinks. The volume of the group was loud. Much louder than the first night in Sorrento. They knew each other now and had common experiences to talk about.

She heard even louder voices at the Park's table and walked over to investigate. A full-on argument was underway between Becca and David.

"I did not take my pill." David was loud and red-faced.

"Yes, you did. Right after you got up from your nap." Becca's voice was meek, and she exchanged glances around the table. It looked to be a repeat of the Monday night disagreement. Mellow felt embarrassed for Becca. Clearly, she was trying to do the right thing.

"Look, I will show you." Becca took the pill container out of her purse and opened up the Wednesday compartment. "See, one pill left. This is for bedtime."

David's reply was loud. "My knee is killing me. Just give me the god damn pill."

Mellow glanced over at Charles and Sharon. They were looking at each other and shaking their heads slowly back and forth.

"Honey, you aren't supposed to be taking these with alcohol, and you are having a martini. I think you should wait."

David snatched the container from Becca's hand. He poured the last pill onto his hand and threw it into his mouth. Then he washed it down with what was left of his martini.

He pushed his chair away from the table. "I am tired, and I am done for the day." He looked over at Becca. "I am going back to the room. Are you coming?"

He didn't wait for an answer, but, instead, began to hobble over to the door.

Becca stood to follow him and looked back at Mellow, "I am sorry, I need to go back with him. He is just not right."

Charles and Sharon both made motions to stand, but Becca stopped them. "No, you two stay. There's no reason you should miss this dinner. I can get him back to the hotel."

Becca then scurried to catch up to David, who had only progressed a few steps away. She put her arm under his elbow to help him to the door.

Charles was again shaking his head and he said to Mellow, "The painkiller that he is taking isn't supposed to be mixed with alcohol. I tried to talk with him about it, but he likes his drinks. Says it makes him sleep better."

Mellow, in spite of her distaste for Becca's infidelity, felt pity for her. Becca seemed to be trying to do the right thing for David, but he was not a cooperative patient. As a Tour Director, this was a tricky medical situation, and she knew she had to stay out of it.

Becca suddenly reappeared. By herself. "Mellow, can I talk with you for a second?"

"Of course." She led her to a more private area of the restaurant.

Becca started, "It's OK. I told him I left my phone on the table."

"How can I help?"

"I am not sure we can continue with the tour. I think we should leave, but I know David will not want to."

Mellow looked her over. Becca's eyes were watering, and she seemed to be on the verge of tears. "Well, Kastner is usually very accommodating for medical situations. I am sure we can work out some kind of arrangement. We are only a third of the way through the tour."

"Can we meet later and talk about this? I need to have a better understanding of how it would work."

"Of course. When would you like to meet?"

"Tonight? Maybe before you go off on the evening event?"

"Sure, we are meeting in the lobby at 9:00. How about you and I talk at 8:15. In the lobby?"

"I'd like some place more private. How about the lower level? They have several conference rooms down there. One has sofas and a table. Can we talk there?"

"That should work. I am really sorry that you are going through this. A European vacation is supposed to be relaxing and fun. And it certainly hasn't been that for you."

Becca said, "Thanks," and she headed off toward the door.

Mellow returned to her group, which was now a little more subdued. The argument between Becca and David took some of the energy out of the group. She circulated among them and, after some effort, she was able to reenergize the discussions. Some had visited the shops on the *Via Condotti*, some had walked to the Spanish Steps, and others just wandered freely. Each had a story and they enjoyed sharing them.

As the 7:00 ending approached, Mark and Victoria came up to her.

Victoria said, "Mellow, this has been a wonderful dinner. So many foods to sample, and all so delicious!"

"But we do have a question," Mark added.

"Sure."

"We are all looking forward to the nighttime tour of the Colosseum. If it is anything like seeing the Trevi Fountain at night, then I am sure we will all enjoy it. But it is late. And many of us are tired. I talked to a few other folks, and we were wondering if we could move it up and get an earlier start?"

Mellow had no objections. It would be dark enough, and she was sure that Angelo could accommodate the change. She quickly scanned the room. All of the guests were still there, except for the Parks. And they weren't going anyway. So, she tapped her water glass and quickly called the group to attention.

"I have had a suggestion that we start a little earlier for our tour of the Colosseum tonight. Is everyone OK with that? Hands up if that's OK with you."

All of the hands went up.

"This way we can all get to sleep a little earlier. How about we meet in the lobby at 8:30 instead of 9:00? I will alert Angelo to the change. We should be back by 10 or so."

She saw several thumbs up and lots of head-nodding.

"That settles it. 8:30 in the lobby."

She knew she had Becca scheduled for 8:15, but she figured that could be a quick conversation. David wasn't getting much out of the tour, and Becca was clearly frazzled. Kastner could offer a partial refund or, once David was up to it, simply add them to a future trip. She just had to get Becca in touch with the guest services staff at Kastner. Her conversation with Becca could be rather quick. She could still be in the lobby by 8:30.

Chapter 32

Rome

Wednesday, May 22, 2019

Mellow was back in her room by 7:30. She had time to check on things, so she took out her iPhone. She scrolled through her emails and found the ones she was looking for. First was from the Avanti Hotel in Assisi, confirming guests, rooms, times, and special accommodations. The group was due to arrive on Friday and Mellow was satisfied that everything was set, including washcloths in the rooms. Next was the restaurant for the Friday evening dinner, *Vivace*. With their email confirmation, they had attached their menu and Mellow quickly reviewed the offerings. It was a great balance of both land and sea, with a mix of light and heavy, and a terrific dessert menu.

It was perfect.

Next, she found the emails from the Florence hotel, where they would arrive on Sunday, and the restaurant for the Sunday and Monday dinners. Again, everything was in order.

Then, she found the email from her local Florence guide. She had worked with Caterina on several tours and knew her well. She was reliable, engaging, smart, and high energy. A far cry from the disastrous Giuseppe. She let out a breath. It looked like the tour was getting back on track. Maybe now she could relax a little bit.

But still no call from Luca. She tapped his number on her iPhone and tried to call him. She had to leave a message.

At 8:00 she decided to walk down to the lower-level conference rooms. She took the steps instead of the elevator. While she was on the last flight down, Luca called.

She answered and hustled into the conference room with the sofas and table. She figured she had a few minutes to talk with him before Becca arrived, so she pulled the door mostly shut.

"Luca, thanks for calling me back."

"Sorry, I wanted to call earlier, but have been tied up."

"I just wanted to give you a heads up on the problem I had with our guide in Rome today."

"What happened? You said that he didn't work out."

"Frankly, he was very rude to one of our guests. He was cracking jokes in the Vatican and one of our guests laughed out loud. So, he proceeded to lecture her, and all Americans for that matter, on how they don't know how to behave."

"Oh, Lord!"

"Yes. So, I took the microphone and his Whispers set and sent him on his way. Right on the spot. I know I don't have the authority to dismiss him, but I told him not to show tomorrow too."

There were several seconds of silence. Mellow decided to wait it out. Finally, Luca said, "Mellow, you did the exact right thing. We can't have that. Our guests come first. I will contact the agency tomorrow and see that he does not work any of tours ever again. But we need a replacement."

"I have one already. She is very experienced and comes highly recommended."

"From the same agency?"

"No. I did not want to contact them."

"Recommended by who?"

"By Aldo." She knew it would have the desired effect.

Luca laughed at the other end of the phone. "Good old Aldo. He is a gem, isn't he?"

"He certainly is. Oh, and there is one more thing."

"What's that?"

"I took over the tour and the guide said that he would report me to the authorities since I am not a licensed guide for either Rome or the Vatican."

Mellow saw the door open slowly and Becca looked in. She waved her to come all of the way in. She held up her finger to signal that she was nearly done.

Luca replied, "Oh brother. He threatened you. I will make sure I mention that when I call his agency."

Mellow felt her phone vibrate and she looked to see that Angelo was calling. "Luca, I have to run."

"I need a few more minutes."

"Sure." Mellow gave Becca a gesture of apology, and mouthed *boss* while she pointed to her phone.

*   *   *

Becca took the far stairway down from her eighth-floor room. This way she could avoid the elevator security cameras. The Lobby ones as well.

She heard Mellow talking in the second conference room, the one that Becca had suggested for the meeting. She leaned close to the door to hear. Mellow was talking on the phone with someone.

The door was closed, but not all the way. She pushed it open and poked her head around the door. Mellow saw her and waved her in. Becca stepped in, closed the door behind her, and leaned against it.

Mellow held up her index finger to signal that she would be finished soon.

Becca reached behind and quietly flipped the lock, moving it slowly to minimize the noise. Mellow, still talking, did not appear to hear the tumble of the lock.

Becca waited. Mellow, so poised and professional, had walked right into this. At the restaurant, Becca had left David at the door and went back to talk with Mellow. "Forgot my phone", she had said. She had rubbed her eyes just before she re-entered the restaurant, then consciously tried to avoid blinking. She had read about this trick online, as a technique that actresses used onscreen when they had to look like they were fighting back tears. Becca had tried it and it seemed to work. After a few moments, she could feel her eyes get watery. The challenge was to control all of the unconscious blinking that people do. But Becca was a master at controlling what she did. And Mellow had fallen for it.

By god, she thought, this is going to work. She felt surprisingly calm. And no guilt whatsoever. The meddling Tour Director had brought this on herself. Becca wasn't worried that Mellow was still talking. There was plenty of time. The drive to the Colosseum wasn't until 9:00.

She put her hand inside her purse and wrapped her fingers around the metal bust.

*   *   *

At 8:15, Mark and Victoria arrived in the Lobby to find that most of the other guests were already there.

He had his phone in hand. Brad Nichols had not called at 8:00 to present the offer for the Baltimore position. Mark figured that he had just gotten tied up in a meeting or a call.

Mark saw Angelo across the lobby, and he thought he looked nervous. He went over to see him.

"Is Mellow here yet?" Mark asked.

"No, not yet. And she is always early. I hope we don't have another incident like the Spanish Steps. Let me call her."

Angelo stepped away to place his call.

Mark heard him leave a voice message. Mark looked around and then back toward the stairway. No sign of Mellow. He walked over to the front desk.

"*Buona sera, signore.*"

"*Buona sera.* We are expecting Mellow, our Tour Director. By any chance have you seen her?"

"I am sorry, sir. I have not."

"*Grazie.*"

"*Prego*"

Mark looked around again and then walked back to Angelo. He spotted Victoria walking over to the piano. He felt a vibration in his hand and checked his phone. A text message from his boss Jerry. *Congrats again. I think the job will be really good for you. Will give you Sales experience. You have a great future ahead of you at LRE!*

Mark read it again. Without being cynical, he was trying to sort out the real meaning. Why would Jerry follow up with a text? Did Mark not show enough enthusiasm in the afternoon call? Jerry was pretty astute, and could tell the difference between genuine and manufactured enthusiasm. The truth was that Mark was still not convinced he needed to do a sales rotation. Jerry picked up on it. But why talk about "great future"? Then, things crystallized in his mind. Jerry was worried that Mark would leave. Mark had taken a day off for his interview in Baltimore. It was his first sick day in a couple of years. Jerry sensed that situation, and figured it out. He was worried about retention. This all meant that Mark could expect a counteroffer, once he gave his notice.

But Brad, the Managing Partner, still had not called to present the other offer. And Paul had said that he was a stickler for time and appointments. Then, while his phone was in hand, he got a text from the Brad: *Sorry, Running late. Can I call you in 5 or 10?*

Wrote back: *Yes. Looking forward to it.*

Mark figured that, once he got the call, he would excuse himself from the evening drive, saying "business emergency". Victoria would roll her eyes, and be annoyed. But, "oh well." She would understand once he explained that it was a job as a president of a business. And future CEO.

Everything was happening at once.

*   *   *

Mellow looked up at Becca. Luca was still talking away in her ear. He said, "I want to talk with you about another opportunity."

Mellow clutched. She figured he had come up with a way to get rid of her without really firing her. No wonder he was being nice.

"OK, what's that?"

"Well, you know that we are always looking for ways to expand the business. One of the plans we have for next year is to expand into the States. We will call it Kastner USA and we are targeting Europeans who want to see the United States. Germans at first."

Mellow again held up her finger to Becca, and then she turned her back and walked a few steps way.

"So how would I fit in?"

"I think you would be great to be on the team that sets it up and runs the operation. You are American, you speak German like a real German, you know our operations, and you have an eye for detail."

Mellow froze. "Wow, I don't know what to say."

"We think it could be based in Washington, D.C. Cover the Capital, of course. Stay on the East Coast to start. Go south to historical sites like Monticello, Mt. Vernon, and Williamsburg. And go north to Philadelphia, New York, and maybe Boston. Our market research says those are the places that Germans would want to see."

"Wow, thanks Luca. This is a lot to think about." Her immediate thought was that it would put her closer to her Aunt Margie in Maryland. And get her back to the States. Her parents house was on the market but hadn't sold yet. She could just move into it.

It didn't sound like he was trying to get rid of her at all. But she wasn't sure what "on the team" meant. How big a team? What would her role be?

"Well, when your group is done, let's meet and talk about it. There is plenty of time."

"Yes, let's do that. I will call you from Venice and we can talk."

"That will work. *Ciao.*"

Mellow returned her own "*Ciao*" and tapped End Call. The clock on her iPhone told her that she was very late for her scheduled time with Becca, so she turned to apologize.

She saw Becca's arm swinging at her and, reflexively, put up her left arm and ducked. She wasn't fast enough. She felt the full blow of a heavy object on her left temple and a sharp pain flashed down the side of her face. Her phone fell several feet away. She crumbled to the floor.

The pain was horrible, and she could feel everything getting dark. She struggled to get up. But couldn't. She collapsed. Unconscious.

* * *

Becca stood over her. "Don't look so helpless. You brought this on yourself. You had to meddle, didn't you? Had to stick your nose where it didn't belong. Had to tell everyone about me and Charles. Well, look at you now."

She walked back to the door and opened it. She checked both directions. Nothing. Then she locked the door again.

Looking over at Mellow's limp body, Becca picked up the metal bust. No blood. Good.

She put it back in her purse and set her purse on the arm of the sofa. Then, she began to drag Mellow's body over toward the coffee table.

"God, you are a little thing, aren't you? I thought it would be harder than this."

* * *

Mark checked his watch. 8:40. He went over to Angelo. "Do you think something is wrong?"

"Let me try her phone again," Angelo said. The call went to voice mail again.

Mark saw tenseness in Angelo's face, and his eyes were busy scanning the floor.

Mark asked, "What should we do?"

"The last time she was late was when she had the problem on the Steps. Let's check her room. She is in 302. Come with me."

Mark heard his phone ring and he felt its vibration. He looked. It was Brad, calling as promised. He looked up at Angelo.

"This is an important call. I really need to take it."

Angelo showed disappointment in his eyes. "Well, you do what you need to do. I think she is in trouble. And needs help."

Angelo waited for several seconds, while Mark stood frozen. His phone rang two more times.

Angelo spun around and started to walk away.

Mark said, "Wait up." As he hustled to catch up to Angelo, he noticed that his phone stopped ringing. It had rolled to voice mail.

*　　*　　*

Mellow could feel a tugging at her body. Agonizing throbs bounced throughout her head. She couldn't focus. Couldn't figure out what was happening. She remembered Becca swinging at her and hitting her with something. Something really hard. Then nothing. Now Becca was dragging her toward the sofa and table. She tried to fight her off, but Becca was too strong. And Mellow too weak.

She felt Becca pick up her shoulders and head. Becca gripped Mellow's head by her hair. She heard Becca say, "Now, let's add to the bump in the same spot."

Her eyes widened as she realized that Becca was going to bang her head against the corner of the table.

*   *   *

The guests were chatting in the lobby. Some anxious. Some not. So what if they were a little late? Maybe something came up? The time had been changed at the last minute. Angelo and Mark will probably find her. It's probably nothing.

Victoria sat at the piano and began to play.

*   *   *

Mellow couldn't sort out what was happening. Becca began to shove Mellow's head to the corner of the table, and Mellow pushed her arm out. Again, pure reflex. The table skidded several inches away and Mellow fell over onto her back.

Becca was on her now, straddling her on both sides. She grabbed Mellow's scarf and began to pull, choking her.

Mellow tried to squeeze a finger under the scarf. But she couldn't.

Becca began to talk wildly. "Don't worry. I will be done soon. Then I can get back to my dead husband. Too many pills, David."

Still choking Mellow, she began to mimic David in the arguments about the pills. "Give me my damn pills."

"No honey. You already had it."

Her voice took on a guttural pitch, "No I didn't. Dammit. Give me my pill."

Now her normal voice, "Well here take another one then. This one will kill you."

"Just give me my damn pills," again a gravelly voice.

Becca switched to a cheerful, sing-song tone. "Sure, here's another. Except this one is mine. Not yours. This one will kill you for sure!"

Mellow couldn't breathe. She was faint, her strength draining. Still couldn't get the scarf off her throat.

She heard her phone ring. Becca, distracted, loosened her grip on the scarf and looked over at Mellow's phone.

Mellow bucked her hips up and knocked Becca off of her. Becca fell over onto the sofa and Mellow started toward the door. She couldn't stand up, so she crawled over. She reached the door and tried to open it.

Locked.

She moved her hand down to the lever to unlock it, but suddenly Becca grabbed her scarf and pulled her away by her neck. With both hands on the scarf, she threw Mellow back toward the sofas. Mellow went tumbling. She struck the arm of the sofa and again fell onto her back. Becca's purse fell off the arm of the sofa and Mellow heard the contents spill onto the floor.

*   *   *

Mark and Angelo knocked on the door to Mellow's room. There was no response.

Mark looked over at Angelo, "Maybe she's in the Lobby now. Took the elevator down, or the other stairway?"

"Yeah, that could be. Let's go back to the Lobby. Maybe she is there waiting for us."

They started down the back stairway. When they got to the Lobby level they started through the door.

Mark heard the piano. Leonard Cohen's "Hallelujah." "That's my mother playing. If Mellow is there, she probably wouldn't be playing anymore."

They looked at each other. Mark wasn't sure what to do next.

Angelo said, "Well, the only other place to look is downstairs."

They headed back to the stairs.

*   *   *

Mellow felt Becca on her again. She was astride her and she had

191

the scarf in both hands. She pulled it even tighter and Mellow felt her neck stiffen. She gasped for breath. But she couldn't breathe. She tried to get her fingers under the scarf, but Becca's grip was too tight. She tried to buck up her hips and knock Becca off. But Becca seemed ready for it, she was sitting higher up on Mellow. Becca started to talk wildly again about giving her pills to her husband and how she would be *free* tonight. Mellow gave up the bucking and started to scratch and pull at Becca's arms. It was no use. Becca wouldn't let up her grip on the scarf. Mellow felt her eyes bulging. Couldn't breathe. The room was again getting dark. There was nothing to do. She felt the presence of her mother. And then her father. It felt like they were waiting for her, reaching their hands out.

Her head fell to the side.

She looked into the face of a metal bust. Marcus Aurelius. It seemed to be saying to her. "Look well into thyself; there is a source of strength which will always spring up if thou wilt always look."

She reached out to the bust, closed her fingers around it, and swung it at Becca's head.

Becca's grip loosened and her eyes fluttered. Mellow pulled the scarf loose and took several coughing, gagging breaths.

Then she pushed Becca's limp body off of her. Still hacking, she crawled to the door. The lock turned easily. She fumbled for the knob and turned it open.

She fell across the threshold as she saw Mark and Angelo running towards her.

Mark got to her first.

"She's in there." Her voice was hoarse and broken. "She tried to kill me."

Angelo ran into the room and grabbed a groggy Becca. Within seconds, he had her in an arm lock and subdued on the floor. He pulled out his phone and began dialing.

Mellow looked up at Mark. "Find her husband." She cleared her throat. "She gave him too many of his pills. And the wrong ones. She is trying to kill him too."

Chapter 33

Rome

Thursday, May 23, 2019

Mellow

Mellow adjusted the pillow in her hospital bed. Her head ached, and even more so whenever she moved. Movement produced shooting pains, not unlike the pains from her fall at the Spanish Steps. She figured if she could get the pillow just right, then her head wouldn't hurt so much. But it didn't help.

She checked the time: 10:15.

She had the window bed in the semi-private room, and, fortunately, the bed by the door was empty. At least she assumed so. The pulled curtain blocked her view, but there was no activity, and no voices, from that side of the room.

Angelo had already come and gone. He brought the Pharmacy Sisters with him, along with Victoria and Mark. They all wanted to check on her before they started their day in Rome. Victoria had said, "We can't pay any attention to anything until we know that you are OK. And that you are going to get through this."

Char had said, "Mellow if you need us to do anything at all, you just let us know. We feel so bad for you."

Mellow was touched by their concern, and the fact that they had taken the trouble to visit her. She felt her eyes watering while she thanked them.

She had asked Angelo about the Parks. He knew that Becca was being held at the station by the *Polizia*. "I called a couple of my *amici* at the station. But the last we have seen or heard about Mr. Park was when he was taken away in the ambulance."

Mark then had filled her in. "After we called for an ambulance for you, we got to the hotel manager to get into their room. He got us in and we called for another ambulance. David was barely breathing."

Angelo picked up the story, "I called Luca late last night. He is having a medical advocate come to the hospital this morning to assist Mr. Park. We got to Mr. and Mrs. Collins as well. They went to the hospital with Mr. Park. I think Aldo went as well."

Mellow had asked about the tour, and Angelo assured her that Luca would have it covered.

Mellow turned her head to look out the window. The day was full of bright sunshine, and she thought that it would have been a great day to see the sights of Rome.

She heard footsteps near the door and turned her head. It was Aldo.

He stood in the doorway and shook his head slowly. "Oh, Mellow."

"Uncle Aldo," her eyes were welling again, "you can't believe how good it feels to see a familiar face."

He came to the chair beside her bed. "How are you feeling this morning?"

"Better, but my head still throbs. The doctor said that the MRI did not show any fractures or bleeding."

"Can you remember things?"

"Yes. Everything. My memory is fine."

Aldo repositioned himself in the chair. His head was down. Mellow thought he looked like a naughty schoolboy getting reprimanded by an authority figure. A teacher? Principal? Parent?

He lifted his eyes, his head still. "Good. Because I have things to tell you that you will want to remember."

"OK. What do you mean?"

He went to the door and closed it. He fumbled for a lock but couldn't find one. Then he made his way back to the chair, glancing at the empty bed.

"I'm glad you have the room to yourself."

Mellow waited for him to continue.

"It is time for me to tell you the truth about your father." He looked at her full on, concern in his eyes. He went on, "I did not sleep last night. I was worried about you, and I was doing a lot of thinking."

Mellow tried to swallow, but her mouth was too dry. "Can I have my water?"

Aldo gave it to her, and she took a long sip from the straw.

"So, you know more than you have been saying." Mellow had always thought that Aldo was holding back. But she had never challenged him on it.

"Given what's happened these last few days, I decided that it would be awful if anything happened to you without you knowing about your father." He let out a slow breath. "If something happened to you before you knew the truth, I would not be able to live with myself."

"Oh boy, what are you going to tell me?"

"First off, you have to promise me that you will not talk with anyone else about this. Or that I told you. We just have to act like we never had this conversation. These things can never be repeated." His eyes focused on hers, "Agreed?"

"OK. Agreed."

"You asked me before about your father being in the CIA."

"Yes, he was given the Distinguished Intelligence Cross. I have a picture. I don't know what he did to get it."

"I am not allowed to talk about it, or say anything. But today I will tell you. You deserve to know."

The ache in Mellow's head seemed to disappear. She was focused on Aldo and what he was saying. Any aches and pains left her consciousness.

Aldo took a momentary glance to the window, as if collecting his thoughts. Then he turned back to Mellow.

"Let me go in chronological order. I worked with him in the 1980s. We were both with our embassies in Bonn. Me for Italy, him for the U.S. The embassies for the old West Germany were in Bonn back then. Not Berlin."

"My father always said that he was a low-level bureaucrat."

Aldo smiled. "He was a whole lot more than that. He was the best agent the CIA had."

"Are you going to tell me who Wilhelm Bauer was, too?" Aldo was taking too long. Mellow had question after question to ask. She wanted Aldo to get to the point.

"Slow down now. Yes, I will get to him."

"OK. I won't interrupt anymore." She wanted to, but she could tell that Aldo was carefully measuring his words.

Aldo looked down and rubbed his palm across his forehead. Then he returned his eyes to Mellow. "Have you ever heard of the Pan-European Picnic. From 1989? You were just an infant at the time."

"Yes, I think so. I have read about it. But I was three years old at the time. My mother and I were back in the States, visiting my grandparents. Dad was in Germany."

"He was not in Germany. He was in Hungary. You have to know that, at that time, Hungary was an Eastern-bloc nation. There was this thing called the Pan-European Picnic, at least they called it a picnic. It was a peace demonstration at the Hungary and Austrian border. Austria was Western-bloc. Thousands of East Germans were there, and Hungary opened up the border with Austria. So, they all fled to the West. From Austria, they made their way to West Germany. In effect the East Germans who couldn't get past the Berlin Wall made their way to Hungary and then to the West."

"So, what did Dad do?"

"He was in charge of the operation. Working behind the scenes of course. Getting people from East Berlin to Hungary. Prepping the Austrians. Getting the Hungarians to stand down."

"How do you know all of this?"

Aldo paused. "I was there. I was working with him."

The two sat in silence for several seconds. Then, Aldo pursed his lips and said, "Let me go on. It was a test. To see how the Soviets would react. Your father was convinced that Gorbachev and the East Germans would be stuck and not really be able to do anything. Gorbachev was sending all of these messages about openness and *Glastnost* and all of that. And your father read the Stasi right by figuring they wouldn't do anything either."

"The Stasi. That's the Secret Police?"

"Yes, it was the old East German Secret Police?" Aldo let out a long breath and looked back at the door. Then, he whispered, "That's where Wilhelm Bauer comes in."

"Huh? Was he in the Stasi?"

"Yes. He was a very high-ranking leader in the Stasi. Your father recruited him as a double agent."

"Recruited?"

"He worked for your father. Wilhelm also monitored the KGB reaction to the picnic. Kept telling us to go ahead and proceed."

"Go on."

"The Pan-European Picnic was just part one. In the Summer. Phase Two was Leipzig. In October."

"What happened in Leipzig? I never heard much about that. Just some big demonstrations or something."

"The critical thing to remember is how tense the situation was back then. Well, you were too little to actually remember. But there were thousands of demonstrators marching against the Communist

Government. In Leipzig. Maybe fifty to seventy thousand. And the Stasi headquarters were in Leipzig."

"What did my father do in Leipzig."

"Let's just say that he … *encouraged* … it. As did I."

"You were there too?"

"Yes. And there were five or six hundred police and Stasi, all with weapons. Loaded and ready to use. People weren't sure if, or when, the shooting would begin."

"OK, obviously Wilhelm Bauer is not his real name. Right?"

"That's right. It was his cover name. Known only to a few people." Aldo paused again. "Wilhelm got the Stasi, and, by extension, the whole police force to stand down and not do anything. If he hadn't, thousands would have died. They were ready to start shooting. Wilhelm prevented it."

Mellow let out a very quiet, "Wow."

"That's why you set off alarm bells when you started calling embassies and consuls asking for Wilhelm Bauer." Aldo put his head back and laughed, "He contacted me when you did that. In a panic."

"Amazing. That explains the picture then too. Dad kept it, maybe I guess as an insurance policy."

"Exactly. I have one too."

"I'm guessing that he is still working as a spy, isn't he?" Her Zurich meeting, or planned meeting, with Wilhelm came to mind. So thorough. So efficient. So invisible.

"He is still very high up in German intelligence. He came to your father's funeral because he had so much respect for him. It was a horrible lapse on his part to use the name 'Wilhelm'. He knows that. It was a terrible slip."

"That explains why all of those Europeans were there."

Aldo nodded a confident *yes*. "Wilhelm would never ever do anything to hurt you. If anything, he is probably looking after you. Making sure nothing happens to you. I am guessing that right now he is checking to see if this wacko woman who attacked you has anything to do with someone's secret police."

"No way."

"Yes, I am sure he is. But let me finish the story. Berlin was Phase Three. We didn't think it would unfold as it did. We were planning for early spring in the next year. But, just after Leipzig, the head of the East German government, Honecker, resigned and we had to move fast. The Wall fell in November."

"Wait a minute. Wait a minute. Are you telling me that my father, you, and this guy named Wilhelm are responsible for the fall of the Berlin Wall?"

Aldo kept his eyes right on Mellow's. "Yes. Hence the Distinguished Intelligence Cross."

Chapter 34

Florence

Three Days Later

The outdoor lunch was a great success. How could it not be? They were in the *Piazza della Signoria*. The sun was shining. A replica of Michelangelo's David was in view at the far end. The splashing water of Neptune's Fountain sparkled in the center of the *piazza*, with the sound providing a soothing background. Just to the side was the imposing equestrian statue of Grand Duke Cosimo I. The food was fantastic, the service flawless.

All of the other guests had left for their afternoon free time, and Mellow was sitting alone with Mark.

Luca, who had flown in from Zurich to cover the tour himself, was off with a group to tour the Uffizi, one of the finest art museums in Europe.

The group was scattered. Some had gone off to the Duomo, others to the jewelry shops on *Ponte Vecchio*, some to the tombs in the *Santa Croce*, and many with Luca to the galleries of the Uffizi. Victoria had left with the North Carolina sisters to shop for scarves, and to visit Mellow's recommended shop for leather coats. Mark had begged off.

Mellow had learned over the years that free time was the best for Florence, as there were so many things to see, and each guest could easily create their own itinerary.

They had a bottle of Brunello on the table, one that Mark had just ordered. He took out his phone and snapped a picture of the label. After a quick search on his Vivino app, he began to tell Mellow about all of its characteristics.

"OK, you can stop right now," she smiled. "I don't care about any of that. I just go by how it tastes."

Mellow adjusted her scarf, making sure it was loose and not knotted. Then she put her head back and closed her eyes. She could finally relax.

Becca was still in Rome, in jail and awaiting court proceedings. They had gotten to her husband David in time, but he was still in the hospital in Rome. Kastner had provided a medical advocate, who was there with him. His lab work had showed that he had toxic levels of an opioid, as well as Clonazepam. The combination was normally deadly. He did not awaken until Saturday, and he was still on a detox regimen.

Mellow herself had spent Wednesday night at the hospital. At Aldo's insistence. She checked herself out on Thursday and joined the group as they drove to Assisi on Friday. Angelo had taken over and managed Thursday, until Luca had arrived.

Luca was proving to be a very effective tour guide. Who would have known?

The whole set of events had made the local press, and social media. Within hours, it was in the U.S. also.

After Mellow informed the *Polizia*, Charles confessed to the affair with Becca. But he was adamant that he knew nothing about Becca's plans. Sharon flew back to the U.S. by herself. Charles was still in Rome. Mellow figured he was torn with guilt and was staying to keep an eye on David. Or trying to avoid going back to the U.S.

Mark poured the wine and offered it to Mellow. She swirled the glass and took a mouthful. She sloshed it around in her mouth and swallowed slowly.

"It's perfect." She closed her eyes again and put her head back.

Mark took one as well. "Yes, an amazing wine." He put his glass down. "You know, if you ever want to get back to the States, you should let me know. I have just accepted a new job, in Baltimore. As the President of a wine importer and distributor. I know lots and lots of people, and I would be happy to set up some introductions."

Mellow opened her eyes and looked him over. He had been very attentive since the incident at the Vatican. He was standing closer and listening more intently. On several occasions, she had caught him looking at her. And she had been genuinely touched that he had gone looking for her at the *Rilassante*. And visited her in the hospital.

She locked her eyes on his. "Baltimore, huh? Now that is really interesting."

Made in United States
North Haven, CT
23 October 2022

25818614R00126